PIRATE OF ATLANTIS

BOOK TWO OF THE EPOS OF ATLANTIS

FENIX HARPER-JONES

Houten & Holleren

EDITIONS

PIRATE OF ATLANTIS
After the translation by
Royce B. E. Gibbons, CMG
retold by
Fenix Harper-Jones

ISBN 979-8-88722-829-7 (e-book)
ISBN 979-8-88722-821-1 (print)
Library of Congress Control Number
2022910789

Art by Ben Tripp

Published by
Houten & Holleren Editions
442 5th Avenue #1682
New York, NY 10018
United States of America
https://houtenandholleren.com/

Dédié à l'aimable Yvette Emilia Maillet

AUTHOR'S FOREWORD

We tend to think that progress is persistent—that is, once a thing has been accomplished, it stays that way. Our recorded history is short enough to support this idea. But look closely and it's clear that mankind is forever starting over.

In 1327, Richard of Wallingford drew plans for an astronomical clock. It measured the phases and nodes of the moon, the height of the tides at London Bridge, and standard and solar time. His design was so advanced that a working example was not completed until twenty years after his death.

Richard of Wallingford at work

He could not have guessed that such a mechanism already existed—1500 years before he was born. In 1901, a fragment of an intricate, geared mechanism of wood and bronze was found off the coast of the Greek island Antikythera. The device had been lost in a shipwreck and buried by tides two centuries before Christ was born.

The Antikythera Mechanism was part of an orrery, or clock of the solar system, and may have had both religious and practical purposes. At the time of its construction, religion and technology served the same gods. It is believed to have accurately predicted the motion of stars and planets.

The technology required to design and build such a device was gained, lost, and regained a millennium and a half later. Modern man has existed for overkull 200,000 years. How often has the tide of progress come in and out during that time?

During January 2020, historic Storm Gloria swept the Mediterranean. Record-breaking waves scoured the western end of the sea. Shallow coastal plateaus were cleared of centuries of sediment, which revealed shipwrecks, artifacts, and ancient villages that had long ago been drowned.

In 2021, French and Italian archaeologists dove a newly-revealed wreck they believed to date from the Minoan period. The remains of the vessel were anomalous—that is, of apparently unique design.

Although analysis will take decades to complete, it is apparent that this ship was already ancient when King Minos built his labyrinth. The cypress wood used in the hull's construction came from trees that were fully grown before the last ice age ended—over 11,000 years ago.

Several bronze objects found inside the wreck are even older—according to radiocarbon analysis, they were fabricated as many as 13,000 years ago. Because these artifacts are much older than the ship, they were likely part of a treasure or collection being transported by their owner when the vessel sank.

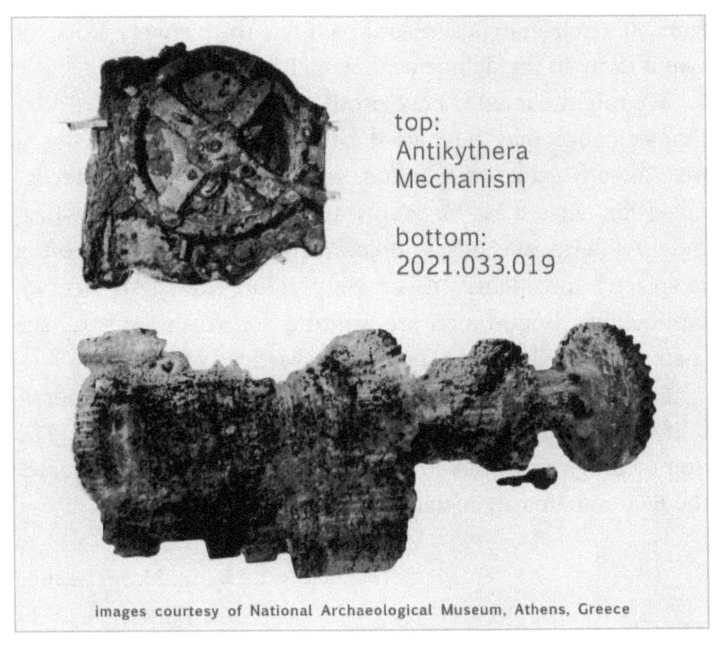

images courtesy of National Archaeological Museum, Athens, Greece

One of the objects, unromantically named 2021.033.019, is reminiscent of the Antikythera Mechanism. It is the length of a man's arm, weighs over 35 kilograms (about 80 pounds), and is made of bronze, copper, and brass. Although profoundly corroded, It appears to be a series of gears along a worm drive shaft, once connected to a larger apparatus.

An intriguing hypothesis claims 2021.033.019 may have been intended to steer a ship along its entire course by mechanical means. If so, the first autopilot was invented when cave hyenas still roamed Europe. The tide of progress comes in and out.

There is no evidence to suggest these fragments of ancient technology are Atlantean in origin. However, they do lend credence to the idea that advanced civilizations could have risen *before* the most recent glacial period, only to be wiped from the archaeological record by miles-thick sheets of ice, or swept away in the deluge as they melted.

We might someday have proof of the *Epos'* Atlantis. Today that evidence may lie buried beneath sea and stone—or it may already have been found, remaining only to be recognized for what it is. Museums are the attics of our civilization. As with any attics, objects stored in them are often misplaced, misidentified, or simply forgotten. Artifacts of incalculable importance are waiting for fresh eyes to see them. Among these may be the last vestiges of Atlantis.

Stranger things have turned out to be true, so the possibility that Atlantis once roamed the seas remains alive. The tide of progress comes in and out. Until proof is discovered, the *Epos* remains an ancient work of imagination.

Fenix Harper-Jones
January 4, 2023

TRANSLITERATION, EPOS OF ATLANTIS

Translation by Royce B. E. Gibbons, CMG

Below is a sample of the literal translation of the *Epos*, without refashioning into poetry or prose. It describes the pirate vessel *Barracuda* after being refitted to replace slave-powered oars with an increased area of sail. Interpretations in parentheses.

Barracuda,
   Three masts
   Triangular Cloth (sails)
   All deck (no benches for oarsmen)
   Three stems (keels)
   [Like] an arrow (in flight)
   Swift (fast, but:)
   Straight (hard to maneuver once launched)

Tar Un Ka yes (Tar Yunkai likes it)
   Stripes Venom yes no (Krait ambivalent about the refit)

Yes no together (they have a love/hate relationship)
   2 kill (together they kill)
   2 rise (together they succeed)
   Yes no together.

PART I

1

———

"I haven't had a crap since we sailed," Krait said.

Tar paused in his axe-sharpening.

"Anything else to report, Skipper?"

"Lookout says he can see warships on the horizon. By tomorrow we'll be rich or dead."

Tar thumbed the edge of the blade.

"Sharp enough for armor," he said.

They stood on the fore quarterdeck of the longship *Barracuda*. A strong breeze hardened the canvas and the sea was lively and green. It was warm weather. Both of them were clad only in loincloths, sword belts, and scars. Her scars were tribal. His came from fighting in the arena as a slave.

"You have to admit," he said, "the extra masts work."

The ship sailed under a new triple lateen rig: three masts, each with a triangular sail mounted to a yard. The central mast was the tallest.

The Barracuda had been completely refitted thanks to her previous captain, Scimi the Black. In accordance with pirate rules, all of his portable goods went to the people who defeated him. These were Tar and Krait, so they co-owned The Barracuda.

They had only known each other for twenty-four hours at the time Krait became captain of the ship. The previous day, she had been in a dungeon awaiting execution, and Tar had been enslaved in the most wretched misery Atlantis could inflict.

They had spent that first day together in uneasy alliance, systematically killing some of the most dangerous opponents in the world on the most dangerous ground in Atlantis.

Tar was a landsman who hated pirates, and Krait was a pirate who hated landsmen. They were still alive because they had trusted each other despite their differences. During the four months since that fateful day, the two of them had been in total opposition at all times, but neither of them gave up the partnership.

"I feel like an asshole sailing this thing," Krait said, appraising the canvas. "We look like a fucking tuna boat. But yes, we are going well fast."

"So my idea was a good one."

"Only because I added a triple keel. Otherwise she'd sail sideways with that much cloth."

The Barracuda was originally a single-deck, thirty-oar galley with a relatively small, square sail. No pirate in their right mind would give up the combined advantage of oars and sails. The problem was that Tar, having been a slave in Atlantis, had committed himself against men owning men.

The slaves who had pulled the oars on their voyage back to land were merely tools to the pirates. But Tar had more in common with them than their masters. He had won freedom at great cost, only to find himself benefiting from the same human bondage he'd tried to escape. That made him *worse* than the pirates, as he saw it.

.   .   .

He had argued the subject with Krait again and again during their voyage to the mainland from Atlantis, but she would not consider freeing the rowers. On the final night before they reached the pirate port of Zanz, so near to land that the night breeze was spiced with the smell of forests, he prevailed.

They were standing beside the Barracuda-headed prow, looking landward. Tar saw only the flash of luminous krill in the water. Krait could see in the dark, but did not share her observations.

"Look, pecker-snot," she said, "I know you were a slave. Sucks a lot. But this is a slave-powered vessel. Those are the slaves. That's just how it is."

"You don't understand what it's like."

"I damn well do," Krait objected. "I was a slave for two months. Two is this many."

She held up two fingers.

"You're wrong," Tar said. "Two is thumbs."

He couldn't count, but used the system of hands common among illiterate and innumerate people in his time.

"Incredible," she muttered. "So what's your solution if we don't have slaves on a slave-powered ship?"

"Make the sailors row?"

"*These* assholes? Seriously? Go ahead and ask. See how you do."

"Put more sails up, I don't care. Rig her like a felucca. They're as fast as anything on the water. But tomorrow when we reach the docks, those galley chains will be struck off."

"You understand we'll have to buy new slaves when we go back to Atlantis? Nothing is gained."

"We're not going back."

"You would lose a thinking contest with a skull. Of course we're going back. I didn't believe the stories of Atlantis's golden roofs and jeweled towers until I was taken there in chains, but it's all true. The whole fucking island is made of treasure. No more shore raids for me. I'm committed to deepwater piracy from now on."

"We'll part in Zanz then," Tar said. He felt bitter.

"That's fucking fine by me. But don't you even think about touching my slaves. These are good ones. I never had premium slaves before. Can't wait to see what they can do in a raid."

"They're half mine," Tar pointed out.

"Not if I kill you."

As his frustration reached its peak, Tar thought of something new. He owned half of the ship, half of the slaves, and half of Scimi's treasure. For the first time in his life, he had something of value with which to bargain.

"I'll give you my half of Scimi's Treasure for the slaves," he said.

"If I thought you were fucking serious, I'd take the deal," Krait laughed.

He offered her his hand. "I'm serious."

She could not resist.

Upon their arrival in Zanz, the slaves were freed. There was no ceremony to it; they were unchained and told to get off the ship. They wandered away in a daze, shaking their heads.

After that, Tar wanted nothing more than to sell his half of the ship and start a new life—if he could find someone to agree to a partnership with this homicidal madwoman. For her part, Krait wanted to kill Tar, take his share of the ship, and keep the slaves.

Neither of them followed through.

Instead, with all of Scimi's treasure to herself, she ordered the Barracuda refitted for sail alone, three-masted like a felucca as Tar had suggested. She paid the crew their back wages and ordered the hold stocked with provisions for a voyage. When that was done, she still had gold enough left over to gamble, whore, and drink herself senseless while the boatwrights did their work.

Tar, on the other hand, was beggared. He had never possessed money before and didn't care about it. It was no sacrifice, in his mind, to give all his riches away in return for the freedom of the galley slaves. But in Zanz, he discovered what money truly represented: everything. While Krait lived like a debauched queen in the best caravansary in town, Tar was sleeping in a ruined hut outside town and eating mangrove lizards to stay alive.

Yet he still believed he'd done the right thing.

"THE PROBLEM," Krait said, "Is that you are the most self-righteous prick of all time."

Tar was drawn back to the present. He had been thinking about the past few months. So had Krait, apparently.

"You're still angry we don't have slaves," he said.

"Fuck off. I admit we are going like a bat out of hell. I admit there are significant efficiencies to be had without slaves. We've got twice the deck and twice the cargo space, we don't have to feed them, and there are no shit buckets to slop out."

"So what's the problem?"

"Without oars, a longship maneuvers like fried ass in close quarters. We *need* the oars. If we had them, we could turn the ship all the way around at a full stop, maneuver fast on a windless day, push off sideways, and go backward or forwards. With sail alone, our choices are fast, slow, or dead in the water. This fucking rig is going to get us killed."

"You lost me at 'close quarters'."

"Weren't you captured by pirates as a boy? Did you not see how we conduct our raids?"

"In my limited experience, you mostly die on the beach. If that's how you conduct raids, it's even more humiliating that I got captured."

"That's your weird Yunkai pride," Krait said. "Nobody of sound mind is embarrassed they got captured. They're sad, scared, and miserable—but not embarrassed."

She spat over the side. Tar punched his fist into his open palm.

"Of course I'm embarrassed! I didn't kill a single pirate and I was the only one captured in my village. I can never go back home. It's better they think I'm dead."

"You were what, thirteen summers old at the time?"

"Both hands, thumbs of another, finger."

He pantomimed the math.

She rubbed her eyes. "You got into a sword fight with a grown-ass professional pirate on a raid, probably high off his tits on jabbo, and you lost."

"As I told you."

"By the clit of the Celestial Hyena—how were you *ever* going to win that fight?"

"What are you getting at? I don't understand."

"There is no child, I don't care what tribe he's from, who can beat a full-sized man who fights for a living. You're not even four hands of years now, and you could kill every child in the world. To think you should have won is so stupid, only you could think it. Now I forgot what I was talking about. *Fuck*."

"You were complaining about close quarters. Why don't you just change tactics?"

"I told you I'm not doing shore runs anymore. That leaves deepwater piracy, which is when you attack a ship, lock on to it, board it, and take it the fuck over. You understand that entire process is close quarters? All of it."

"What's a large number?"

"A thousand? Why."

"There must be a thousand ways to take a ship."

"There's *one*."

"Think of one more. Nobody will expect it."

Tar walked away. He went up the mainmast to take a shift on watch, perched on the padded crossbar near the top. Already he could scamper up the rigging like a spider. He had the makings of an able sailor.

Today, Krait thought, *is the day I throw him overboard.*

She thought this every day.

"Skipper Krait, Ma'am?"

It was one of Scimi's old crewmen, Hotto the Bee. He'd gotten the name by fighting a sea battle with a 'sting'—an arrow stuck in his buttock. He was holding a bedraggled, greenish-faced man by the cowl of his bilge-soaked cloak.

Krait turned her irritation on the seasick stranger. "I'm in a stabbing frame of mind. Who is this peckeroon?"

"Pendrax Turin of Men," the man croaked.

Hotto cuffed him on the head.

"He says his name's Pendrax Turin, Skipper."

"And how the fuck came he here?"

Pendrax, a quick learner, kept silent.

"I smelled puke belowdecks," Hotto said. "But none of us is pukers, so I looked around and found him hiding behind the big fish pots."

She laughed. Her laugh always sounded like a threat.

"A stowaway! Why is he here?"

Hotto cuffed Pendrax again.

"Why are you here?"

"I must reach Atlantis," Pendrax said.

"He says—"

"We're not going to Atlantis. First make him clean up the

vomit, then throw him to the lion shark that's been following us."

Hotto shook Pendrax by the neck. "You heard the Skipper."

He cuffed him once more, out of habit.

TAR DESCENDED the rigging and met them on the way to the hatch below.

"I'll see to him," he said to Hotto.

The sailor looked nervously up at the vacant masthead.

"But then, who's on watch?"

"You are."

The space below deck was too low to stand up straight, and tall enough so that everyone walked around bent double rather than crawling. There was a good deal of empty cargo room, to be filled with plunder from the ships they raided. Pendrax had hidden behind the enormous clay jars because there was nowhere else that offered reliable concealment.

Tar did make Pendrax clean up the mess. The man scrubbed vigorously, to his credit. Tar settled comfortably on a sack of beans and supervised. He was glad to be out of sight of the crew. They were still upset with him concerning the galley slaves. It also interested him to meet someone who was eager to go to Atlantis, rather than flee it.

"It's a terrible place," Tar said. "A thin layer of gold over a rotten whale carcass."

"I come and go. My interests are quite specific," Pendrax said.

"Are you from there?"

"No, I'm from Okré, a mainland nation subject to Atlantean rule. It lies between the Depa-Hu River and the Island of Marka, near the equator."

"Are you loyal to Atlantis?"

"It pulled my homeland out of barbarism."

Tar scratched his chest, considering that answer. It wasn't a real answer at all.

"So why did you go to such lengths to get there?"

"I am a doctor. She has the greatest medical library in the world."

"Medicine in books." Tar had never thought of that before.

"In books and in person. My master is Sept-Ru, House Tanka. He was healer to High Priest Grawa of Atlantis."

"Your master? I thought you were a freeman."

"I *am* a freeman. My caste is Ba-Paridra. But freemen also have masters."

Ba-Paridra was one of the higher castes, fifth from the top —a hand, by Tar's reckoning. To learn that upper-caste freemen also had masters was horrifying to him. Was no one in Atlantis truly free? He dismissed the subject. What mattered was that Pendrax was a healer.

"Throw that bucket overboard," Tar said. "I need to speak with the captain."

2

"**Y**ou have gone too fucking far this time," Krait said. Draw sword, you caitiff turd!"

Tar ignored the hook-backed cutlass she thrust at his face.

"Do we have a healer on board?"

"No!"

"This man is one."

"We don't *need* a doctor," Krait raged. "There's plenty of sea to bed the wounded. Come on, draw!"

He had pushed to the limit of her patience with his latest request. Between that and the constipation, she might finally snap. But it was too late to back down.

"No," he said.

"Then I'll fucking kill you where you stand."

"You won't."

Tar was sure she wouldn't kill him. With his reflexes, he could put his sword through her heart before she knew he'd drawn. She may have come to that same conclusion, or she may have considered the advantages of a healer on the

Barracuda. Whatever her reason, she thrust the cutlass back under her sash.

"Only piss-yellow cowards crew a healer," she said. "He's your responsibility. If he fucks up, you give me your half of the Barracuda."

"It's a deal," Tar said.

He knew this was another terrible negotiation. If the healer did betray him, Tar resolved he would make the man cook and eat his own testicles, and that they would still be attached to his body throughout the ordeal.

"By the way," he added, "this may not be a good time, but I thought of another way to take a ship. In the fighting pit, I fought in a reenactment of the Red Tempest battle. There were miniature warships, and—"

"If you did it in the fucking arena, it wasn't a real naval battle," Krait grunted.

"You're right. It wasn't real. That's what gave me the idea."

He kept an eye on her sword-arm and told her his plan.

PENDRAX HAD STOWED AWAY with ease. He had walked onto the unguarded Barracuda the night before she sailed, while the entire crew was drunk in the Forest Pig tavern. Pirates never got stowaways—the thought didn't even occur to them.

What he hadn't anticipated was how sickening the voyage would be. He'd never traveled before in anything smaller than a three-tiered passenger ship. The narrow space under the Barracuda's deck, lightless and stuffy, was the worst possible berth for a man who hadn't felt the roll of a shallow hull.

Now he sat cross-legged in the clean salt air, wolfing down

flatbread with dried fish soaked in wine. He felt much better. The sun was setting on the ocean, glazing the ship with golden light. He was at the stern near the steersman, who kept the ship on course by levering the long tiller that operated the rudder.

The steersman sang one of the rowing songs sailors called wails, which typically evoked the perils of seafaring life. Pendrax had never heard these before.

> Pull the oar, boy, pull the oar
> The mainland's getting near
> There's the shore, boy, there's the shore
> And all that we hold dear
>
> She wallows in the swells, boy,
> For the hull's been breached
> So you'll paddle like hell, boy,
> 'Till she's safely beached!
>
> Pull the oar, boy, pull the oar
> The mainland's getting near
> There's the shore, boy, there's the shore
> And all that we hold dear
>
> Now she's sinking faster, boy,
> The water's at her deck
> If you'd escape disaster, boy
> You'll paddle at my beck!

After two more verses, the vessel in the song sank, and everybody drowned within hailing distance of dry land. The steersman thoroughly enjoyed the singing of it.

To Pendrax there were many mysteries surrounding the Barracuda. Where were the slaves and oars? Why was she masted like a game-fishing boat? And who were these two that disagreed about everything, yet were partners in fortune?

He also wondered at the liberty he'd been given. He expected to be confined again, or shackled at least, but instead had free rein about the ship. Nobody took the slightest interest in him.

They were all preoccupied with some scheme invented by Tar Yunkai. Strange preparations had been going on all day. The large, lidded clay pots behind which he had stowed away were brought up on deck. The dried fish was dumped out onto a spare sail, then bundled away below deck again.

Sailors smeared the insides of the pots with pitch. There was always a supply of the stuff on any ship. It was used to seal the joints in the hull planking and weatherproof the ropes.

Other sailors removed the deck planks around the masts and down the central gangway, leaving only the fore and aft quarterdecks in place.

Another team stripped the sails from the mainmast, then hoisted the mast out of its socket by means of winches in the tops of the fore and aft masts. Once its base was clear, they belayed the mainmast in position with opposing ropes. It hung in midair, as steady as if it was still firmly plugged into the hull. The mainsail, meanwhile, was lowered alongside to soak in the ocean.

Was this some kind of theatrical performance put on for Pendrax's sole benefit, or had the pirates all gone mad?

During these preparations, Tar Yunkai went about stacking weapons along the gunwales and distributing baskets of arrows. This alone told Pendrax that the work ahead was in deadly earnest.

When the preparations were done, Captain Krait shouted for everyone to assemble. They gathered at the stern, the crew standing in the now-exposed bilges, their unusual leaders standing on what remained of the afterdeck.

"Hear me!" Krait shouted.

"Aye, Skipper!" two dozen voices replied.

Pendrax was surprised to see that about a third of the Barracuda's crew was women. Women didn't fight or sail in Okré.

"You know pirating is mostly a shore-hugging business," Krait said, "but it's gotten so there are more fucking patrol boats than plunder in the shallows. Nowadays, the best pickings are on the open water between the coast and Atlantis. By the greasy crack of the Blue Virgin, it's time we hunted there!"

The crew agreed vocally with this bold idea.

"Before morning comes," Krait said, "we're after a bireme of fucking war. With her under our control, we can pick off merchant ships. They'll welcome us alongside with open arms. We'll strike the bireme in the darkest hour, and attack according to Chief Dickwit's plan. Understood?"

"Aye, Skipper!" came the collective reply.

"Then edges sharp, arrows true, and let's fuck that big-arsed bitch of a warship."

3

———————

That night, nobody slept. As the Barracuda cruised toward the bireme Krait had selected, the crew found small tasks to occupy themselves. Krait, whose sexual appetites peaked before a fight, entertained several of her sailors on the foredeck—male and female alike. They swallowed live peffs, tiny silver fish that secreted poison. Unfortunately for these fish, the poison produced a voluptuous euphoria in humans.

Ignoring the rhythmic snarls of ecstasy, Pendrax watched Tar circulate around the deck from one group of sailors to another. He had lengthy discussions with them, with much gesturing to clarify his points.

He was reviewing their roles in the upcoming attack, Pendrax guessed. It seemed there was a part for everyone to play in the pit-fighter's strategy.

THE WEEK before he boarded the Barracuda, Pendrax had spent many nights and a great deal of money in the taverns of Zanz. Sailors were notoriously indiscreet when drunk, so he bought the drinks. In return, he learned a great deal about pirates, and particularly pirate captains.

It became clear that only Krait Venom of the Libagoro had the skills—and madness—for the work he had in mind. That she was partnered with the man Pendrax recognized as the Golden Prince only reinforced his decision. They were both geniuses, in their own terrible ways.

That was the true reason he'd chosen to stow away aboard the Barracuda. He was indeed a doctor, and a good one. The library he'd spoken of was the best in the world. But this mission was well outside the scope of that career. It had been given to him by someone whom he could not refuse.

Hiding behind the fish pots in the hold, he'd wondered why the first two days of sailing had been so sickening. The long, rolling swells had turned his guts inside out. After he was dragged up on deck for the first time, he saw the reason why: they had sailed far from shore, almost halfway to Atlantis. Pendrax's original scheme was supposed to unfold near the mainland. In the middle of the ocean, it would be much harder to execute—if not impossible.

To succeed, he was going to need the trust of both Krait and Tar. The pending battle might be his chance, or it might be the end of his mission and his life.

He was beginning to doze when there came a sharp cry. He awoke instantly, thinking Krait had decided to kill him after all. It was still dark, the crisp, white stars having rotated a few degrees across the sky. He saw that the dangling mainmast had been clothed in sail again, but was not rigged. It hung like a wet shirt on a line.

Bare feet were thumping back and forth across the deck. More voices joined in the shouting. Every lamp aboard was snuffed out. First Mate Skraj thrust an axe into his hands in the darkness.

"Be ready to fight for your life," the pirate said, and hurried away down the deck to his assigned position.

A team of sailors was splashing seawater everywhere, forming bucket chains in well-drilled order. Pendrax got a full measure of water across his back. It seemed they intended to wet down the entire ship.

The crew hurrying around him were dark patches in a dark world. Pendrax could see little but the flicker of phosphorescence in the wake that stretched out behind the ship, and the black outline of the sails against the stars. The others didn't need light in a place so familiar. They knew the entire craft by feel.

He hadn't been awake for more than three minutes before every sailor was crouched under the starboard rail, as if they were keeping out of the wind. Many had round bronze-clad shields slung on their backs. Others wore helmets with studded leather capes attached. Their weapons glinted dully in the starlight.

Only one figure could be seen moving on the deck, striding up and down. Pendrax strained his eyes but could not see who it was. Then she spoke. It was the captain. Her voice was harsh and eager.

"I make her for our man o'war," she said. "Beakhead on the prow and two sets of oars—a bireme for sure. Any of you squid-cocks see different?"

"I don't see a perishing thing, Skipper," someone replied.

"She's got the eyesight of two owls put together," said another. "Remember that when you're having a wank in the dark!"

A guttural laugh went up along the rail.

Pendrax looked over the side, searching the darkness. He saw nothing, not even the horizon.

"Have they seen us yet?" asked another of the crew.

Someone down the row farted loudly.

"I reckon they've smelled us!"

The laughter faded away as the Barracuda knifed through the dark sea toward its quarry.

Tar and Krait were now in constant motion, checking their preparations again and again. Everyone aboard knew the role they would play, and the roles of the sailors next to them. Some of them would die. Others would have to take over their part in the action.

At last, there was nothing left to do but wait. Even in the face of death, the entire crew was eager for the fight. The monotony of sailing made the sailors wild for action. The more blood they spilled, the richer they'd be. And if it was their blood spilled instead, well—

None of them ever completed that thought. It would be someone else's blood tonight.

THE PRESENCE of death sharpened the mind, Tar knew. But there wasn't any point in dwelling on whose death it would be. His Gods chose who won and lost with dice made from human skulls—and cheated, as often as not.

"Ever had this fucking stuff?" Krait said.

Tar had been staring into the darkness beyond the rail. She appeared beside him with a small container carved from a whale's tooth.

"Is that jabbo?" he asked.

"That's right. Nose lightning."

She tapped a pale green powder into the hollow at the base of her thumb and snorted it up her nostrils, one at a time.

"Hoooaaaah!"

Then an explosion of sneezing took her. She doubled up and gripped the rail. She was grinning so hard Tar could see her entire teeth. She glared out into the darkness with eyes the color of raw meat.

"You've got snot on your face," Tar observed.

"And I pissed myself," she said. "Honk some boner dust?"

"I'll try it another time," Tar said.

A bright yellow rocket flare shot into the night sky. Krait's pupils were dilated beyond their natural limits. Tar could see the back of her eyeballs in the flarelight.

The rocket went up less than a mile distant. The Barracuda was starkly visible in the glare, shadows bending as the fireball scribed an arc across the stars.

4

———

Pendrax saw the Barracuda's fish-pots full of pitch, the mainmast suspended on its ropes, and the pirates hunched under the margins of the deck. They were in the most gleeful of spirits, not least because they were passing snuff boxes of jabbo up and down the line.

"Is that a fire-catapult?" Pendrax shouted. The reality of their danger cast all else from his mind. Suddenly his mission was forgotten.

A heavy hand fell on his shoulder. Tar had found him by the light of the fireball.

"A sun rocket," Tar said. Every fighting ship has a set. Yellow means they've sighted us."

Skraj broke in with a bit of call-and-response song, and others took it up with him:

"What say the flare's winking?" he began.

The others took up the chorus:

> "To see by is yellow
> And red's the alarm
> Blue is for shallows

And green is for calm.

"Red over yellow
Says you're in pursuit
Blue over red
You're changing your route—"

There were more verses dealing with the meaning of every combination of flares. The last one was for disasters:

"By foes or bad weather
If scuttled you be,
All flares together:
Fly hither to me!"

After that, the half-mad crew began singing whatever tune popped into their heads—mostly ditties about battles, suffering, and death, which improved their spirits even more. Krait joined in the songs, clashing two cutlasses together for rhythm. Tar did not share their enthusiasm. He took Pendrax's chin in his hand to focus his attention.

"Get your head in the arena, Pendrax. I put what healing supplies we have under the stern deck. Take off those sleeves. There's blood coming. If you can save a single life, you'll be the equal of anyone aboard this ship. I promise you that."

It wasn't a tempting offer, but it was exactly what he required. Pendrax made his way to the tail of the boat, where enough of the aft quarterdeck remained to form a sheltering roof. He crawled underneath it as the glare of firelight fell into the sea and winked out.

"Here come the stiff-necked geese," shouted the captain, and stepped behind the foremast.

Pendrax heard a sound like rustling grasses in the breeze. It grew louder as it came closer.

A cracking volley strafed the entire ship from end to end. The sea all around splashed and spat as if swarming with fish.

Something struck the deck directly above Pendrax's head. He reached up in the darkness and his fingers found an arrow shaft, still quivering from the impact, the razor-edged head buried in the planks.

His heart began to hammer his ribs as if it intended to break out and jump over the side. He might do so himself. Surely the water—teeming as it was with vicious carnivores —would be safer than the deck? Better to drown than die studded with arrows.

More shafts smote the boards around him. His all-important mission, which had sustained him through every danger so far, completely left his mind. He was nothing more than a monkey looking into the eyes of a jackal.

When he tried to move his legs, they would not respond. He was too afraid even to crawl deeper under cover. He clutched the axe he'd been given and tried to remember the prayers of his people, but could only recall the names of the bones in a human foot. So he recited those, then the bones of the hand, vertebrae, and skull.

"Distal phalanx, then proximal phalanx, sesamoids, first metatarsal... "

"Hold your places!" shouted the first mate.

"... Medial cuneiform... "

"Healer!" Tar barked.

A man was groaning with agony somewhere down the line. The sound broke through the paralysis of terror. Pendrax was a doctor. Cries of pain were the song of his craft. He crawled toward the wounded man. Even as he did so, the air was filled with that terrible rustling and whispering from above. Another flight of arrows was coming.

And this time, they were on fire.

The flaming arrows set the foresail ablaze, bristled from the masts, and studded the deck and hull with fist-sized fires. One of them went through Pendrax's sleeve. He tore off the flaming linen. The captain strode around stamping out the flames with her bare feet.

"Drop that sail!" she shouted. Three sailors leaped up at her command. One of them was struck dead with an arrow through his ribs. The others got the blazing sail down and tossed it into the waves.

To Pendrax's surprise, the ship didn't ignite. He understood why they'd soaked the entire vessel with water. Now that he could see by the firelight, he went to the wounded man, but he'd since been pierced by several more arrows. He was dead.

There was a woman with a shaft through her elbow. He crawled to her side.

"Come aft with me," he said.

She followed, keeping low. No arrows had struck the deck for half a minute. Another flight could rain down at any moment. Pendrax opened the Barracuda's medicine chest. It was rudimentary at best, but there was plenty of linen for bandages, and a few ill-assorted tools he could adapt for purpose.

He began to work on her wound. The arrow had passed in and out of the flesh in the crook of her arm, at such an angle that it had done no great damage.

"Unless you have something better to do," he said, clipping the arrowhead off with a hoof-trimmer, "I'm going to need your help tonight."

"No problem," the pirate said through gritted teeth. "But I ain't gonna fuck you."

Pendrax took a final look down the length of the Barracuda. Two sailors lay dead in the bilges. The suspended mainmast with its drooping triangle of sail resembled a skinned carcass hung up for butchering. Only the rearmost sail held any wind, but momentum carried the Barracuda along its course.

Krait, standing on the deck in full view, could have been a warrior queen. She wore a close-fitting steel cap with gold-chased cheekpieces, a breastplate carved with intertwined golden snakes, and a skirt of studded leather strips.

Tar, moving among the crew, wore only his loincloth, sash, and a pit-fighter's steel *manica* and *galerus* to protect his sword arm and shoulder. He was delivering last-minute instructions and making sure someone took the place of the wounded in his scheme.

The enemy vessel came looming into view over the starboard side like a thundercloud. Pendrax's forgotten childhood prayers all came back to him at once.

5

It was a big warship, a bireme twice as tall as the
Barracuda and half again as long. Two banks of oars
were thrust through her bronze-plated hull like quills
on a porcupine. The upper deck was lined with heavily-
armored men standing at the ready, flaming arrows nocked to
their longbows. Torches were set in brackets along the rail.
They cast monstrous shadows on the warship's square
mainsail.

"One more fucking volley," Krait shouted, her voice as
bold and assured as if they were winning. "Take it in the ass
like a blowsabella, then we put on our show."

When the next volley came, Pendrax only caught the
whistling sound for a moment before blazing arrows
hammered the boards above his head. He involuntarily threw
himself down, across the breast of a grizzled sailor with a
wounded leg.

Towers of red fire leaped up from the Barracuda's hold.
Pendrax cried out with terror.

"It's all part of the plan, lad," said the old sailor, and
patted his arm. "Now get off me. I ain't gonna fuck you."

What happened next was a blur, glimpsed from the corners of Pendrax's eyes as he worked to repair increasingly dire wounds. Within minutes he had collected seven patients, all stuffed into his low shelter.

He saw that the fires, which he thought were feeding on the hull, were confined to the clay fish pots. The pitch burned spectacularly, but at no cost to the ship. He saw the crew crouched at the ready, armed with bows, knives, axes, and swords. They wore the armor of twenty different tribes and nations. Their faces were mad with rage and joy at once.

"Cut!" Tar shouted.

Sailors chopped the lines that held up the now-flaming mainmast. It toppled like the tree it had once been, splashing into the ocean, the sail billowing in the swell like an underwater cloud.

A shout of triumph came up from the enemy ship, so near that Pendrax could hear individual voices among the soldiers on its deck. The warship towered over the gunwale before scraping alongside. The Barracuda shuddered and groaned with the impact. Grappling hooks clattered down from the warship and pulled fast, roping the vessels together. Scaling nets followed. Armed men began to swarm down the nets.

Tar and Krait bellowed at the same moment:

"Lights out!"

Sailors clapped lids on the pots of flaming pitch. The dazzling fires were snuffed. The Atlantean men swarming over the side of the warship were blinded by the sudden darkness—and that is when the pirates struck.

No further orders were needed. The pirate crew fired a volley of arrows near point-blank into the dark, then leaped up and hurled themselves at the boarding nets. For a long while there was only the sound of bloody combat.

While Pendrax struggled to keep a fork-bearded man from bleeding to death—an arrow had passed clear through his neck—his ears were filled with screams and clashing of steel. The furious din came from overhead, battering back and forth. Blood-mad fighters pursued, fled, rallied, and hacked, spilling bodies over the sides. Pendrax heard wounded men drowning, then dying in the jaws of sea-tigers and sharks attracted to the blood.

He lost track of time and forgot even the battle, doing everything he could to keep death away from his ever-increasing heap of patients. He stopped trying to repair the wounds, and sought only to stop the bleeding. Time enough for stitches if any of the Barracuda's complement survived until dawn.

That included him. He didn't hold much hope for his survival.

He kept pulling out arrows and lashing fish-mouthed wounds together. Corpses of those whom he could not save lay across his feet as if he'd cut them down with his own axe.

He saw one more glimpse of the battle, looking up from his work to wipe the blood from his eyes: men were slaughtering men on the warship's deck, high above. The broad square sail was on fire, forming a hellish backdrop. Silhouetted against the blazing canvas were Krait and Tar.

She made a cage of glittering steel around her with a sword in each hand, slashing an Atlantean soldier to ribbons. At her back, Tar's axe stove in the helmet of another as he crushed the throat of a third with his fist.

Pendrax had seen enough. It wasn't their proficient butchery that made him look away—it was the glee on their faces.

6

An hour or a year from the moment the fire-pots went dark, there came a shout from the deck above, a weary but triumphant howl. The battle was won. Which side prevailed, Pendrax could not guess.

Then Tar's voice carried above the rest.

"Give up your arms and you will be spared!"

Krait was next.

"What? Fuck no, we kill them all!"

Then there was an argument.

At length, Tar's voice was raised again.

"Slaves! Join us and get *paid* to row. What say you?"

There was a brief rumble of talk, and then a hoarse cheer came up from the warship's benches.

The battle was over.

The sashes of the dead were collected and their corpses were thrown overboard. Makeshift repairs were performed on both ships.

Meanwhile, three stout landing canoes were lowered from the captured battleship. Into them climbed the surviving Atlantean soldiers and officers. Most of the warship's sailors remained behind. They came from all over the world, and few had any particular loyalty to Atlantis. Only the native Atlantean sailors chose to leave.

The Atlanteans expected to be shot for sport in the canoes. Pirates only spared their victims as an observance on certain holy days, the next of which was six weeks away.

Instead, sacks of dried fish and casks of water were tossed down, and the sailors who remained behind began introducing themselves as the Atlanteans paddled away and were lost to view beyond the swells. The sky was filling up with rosy daylight. The sea glowed as if the horizon were made of molten gold.

Strangers who had traded murderous blows an hour earlier now exchanged sheepish greetings. Old comrades from previous cruises rued what harm they'd done to each other, then embraced.

Those who did not know each other compared the embroidery on their sashes, like fishwives admiring each other's aprons.

By the stitching they could see which ships and captains they had in common, which routes they'd sailed, how many times they'd been to Atlantis and crossed the equator, and what port they called home. A sailor's biography was knotted around his midriff. In this way, men and women who had never met discovered how their lives intersected.

That was also why survivors collected sashes from the dead—to send them to their home port, so their people would know the story of those whom they had lost.

Pendrax continued working to keep sailors and sashes together. His impromptu surgery was expanded around him while he labored. Tables were made of deck boards and sailors helped him with the lifting and holding down of writhing wounded. Others stitched up wounds—every sailor knew how to sew.

At last, bloody as a mammoth-butcher, Pendrax had finished the most urgent interventions. Who lived or died was out of his hands. The Gods would decide whom they took.

He knelt on his aching knees in the crimson bilge, exhausted. He was flooded with relief such as he'd never felt before. Alive and unhurt after a naval battle—in which he had been, by a twist of fate, on the side of the pirates. His mission had taken him on adventures no one could have anticipated. That he was still alive renewed his sense of purpose.

He saw that Tar was nearby, stained red from head to foot, his lion-yellow eyes fixed on the row of crudely-doctored sailors. The pit-fighter's own flesh was scored with fresh cuts. He seemed not to feel pain.

"You've had a fine fight," he said to Pendrax.

The healer nodded. He was too weary to speak.

"Krait!" Tar shouted.

The pirate captain appeared at the rail of the hulking warship above.

"I'm busy, you asshole," she said, affectionately.

Tar indicated the wounded.

"Look. They might be dead without the healer."

"They're just going to be fucking useless for a few days and die of infection."

She went back to her business aboard the warship.

Tar walked among the wounded now. He spoke words of encouragement to those who were conscious:

"That will leave a fine scar to impress your bastard children back in port… How are you going to count without all your fingers? …One eye is as good as a pair. "

Pendrax's newly-alive mind was seething with questions. He struggled to decide which were the most important.

"Tar Yunkai," he said, "what happens now?"

Tar looked admiringly up at the prize of the battle.

"Now we use this fine Atlantean ship as bait. She's called the *Cormorant*."

"How did a small crew like yours defeat such a formidable opponent?"

"Surprise. As far as the Atlanteans knew, our hull was burning and our mainmast was lost. They thought the battle was over when we hadn't even begun."

As he spoke, sailors were guiding the dripping mainmast back into its socket. Others were re-laying deck planks across the thwarts, sealing up the hold once more. Although it looked as if they would be pulling arrows out of the woodwork for weeks, there was no serious damage to the Barracuda.

"But that ship is four times the size of yours. You were outnumbered."

"Atlantis isn't at war right now, so it sends these warships out with the minimum crew to sail them, and a token number of soldiers. Their only purpose is to remind us who rules the seas, not to fight. That's why we dared take her."

"Her complement wasn't more than two hands of hands aboard," said Lumba, one of Pendrax's less-injured patients. He had lost an ear during the battle.

"Didn't you say your mother gave you those earrings, Lumba?" Tar asked.

"She's going to be furious I lost one."

The bloody fighters laughed.

"So this was all to your plan," Pendrax said to Tar. He was impressed, despite his distaste for it all. "What do you do now?"

"We sail this fine warship up to another one like it and add it to our fleet."

7

———

The wounded recovered or died over the next few days, mostly according to luck. Pendrax could only monitor their condition and change dressings. The medicines aboard the Barracuda were limited to what commonplaces the sailors knew how to apply. They had never before attempted to save the grievously wounded, and weren't equipped to do so. At the end of the third day following the seizing of the Cormorant, three sailors remained between life and death.

Only their survival kept Krait's dagger out of Pendrax's neck. She didn't like doctors in general, and she specifically didn't like him. In addition, Tar had freed the Cormorant's galley slaves before they so much as raised an oar, and had convinced her to let three canoes of prisoners go free. She was in a piss-poor frame of mind. A stabbing might improve it.

THE TWO VESSELS sailed in formation, the Cormorant in front, the Barracuda close behind. The warship concealed the smaller craft from Atlantean eyes. They followed the course marked on the charts that had been given to the Cormorant's recently-deposed commander, so that no one would suspect she was under new management. As soon as they captured another bireme, the real fun would begin.

With two warships and the Barracuda, they'd be unstoppable. They could blockade a port city and demand outrageous sums to go away. Tar had one in mind—Khatha, where Scimi had once lived. It was decadent and poorly defended. Krait rarely agreed to his ideas without a fight, but she liked the idea of extorting their late mutual enemy's hometown.

"Maybe we can seize Scimi's property there as well," Krait mused.

"Not likely," Tar said. "I burned it to the ground when I was a child."

THE CORMORANT'S masthead was near twice the height of the Barracuda's, and afforded an excellent view of the horizon. On the fourth day, the lookout atop the Cormorant spotted a sail at the very edge of the world. It was another warship like herself.

Tar and Krait planned to attack it in two days. For now, there was little to do but wait; they spent the time on repairs to both ships, and even stopped a while so the grimy crews could bathe in the sea.

Krait was growing more and more restless, and was clearly fixated on finding a pretext to kill Pendrax.

Having been the object of her bloodlust many times, Tar felt a certain kinship with anyone whom she wanted to kill. The healer was a well-educated man with wide-ranging knowledge. He knew as much about repairing the body as Tar knew about damaging it, and was versed in court life, history, geography, and many more diverse subjects. He reminded him of old Eregin, the Atlantean teacher of etiquette who had taught Tar the rudiments of polite behavior.

The two-ship pirate convoy sailed parallel to the distant warship's path. When night fell, there was nothing to be done except wait for daylight to pick up the stalking.

The night of the sighting, The crew sat in scattered groups around the decks and drank biridi, the powerful twice-distilled sugarcane wine beloved by all seamen. They played the popular dice game 'red and blue', whittled ivory, or sewed canvas by the mingled light of the quarter moon and cresset lamps. The sailors sang their chanties, voices drifting away over the wine-dark sea. Sometimes the giant whales would reply with their own keening melodies.

Tar and Pendrax sat apart against the gunwale and shared a jar of biridi. The healer enjoyed talking, but Tar observed there were certain subjects of which he did not speak. He spoke of his master, but never named him. He spoke of his profession, but never his family. Obsessed as people were with status and bloodlines in the Atlantean world, this was unusual.

It was obvious the man hadn't stowed away to get to some library on Atlantis, as he claimed. In Tar's estimation, he had all the marks of a fugitive looking to start his life over. Now he had a new life, plugging the holes in wounded sailors.

Tar was surprised when Pendrax spoke like a pirate for the first time.

"I don't know why you're going after those warships," the healer said. "They've nothing of value aboard."

That was the sort of thing a buccaneer would think about.

Tar shrugged. "The cargo doesn't matter. It's the ships we want."

"But you're pirates. It seems to me you'd be hunting the treasure barges, not some floating barracks."

Tar shook his head. "We're bold, not stupid."

"I'm surprised, that's all. Your captain Krait seems like the sort to attempt the impossible."

"Nothing she loves better. But as I say, we have other plans."

"Which are?"

"None of your concern."

"Then tell me, what's wrong with treasure barges?"

"Where do I begin? They're bristling with harpoon crossbows. They're double-hulled and unsinkable. Each of those ships carries a platoon of warriors. Even if you got aboard, they're full of locked doors and ironclad holds."

"Yes, but—"

Tar wasn't finished.

"That's to say nothing of their escort ships, the triremes. One in front, one in back, and one on each side. Deadliest ships in the Atlantean navy. Big as fortresses, with ballistae, fire and glass catapults, harpoons, grappling guns, and steel rams as long as the Barracuda herself. If we had a fleet of Cormorants, we still couldn't win. *That's* what's wrong with treasure barges."

"It's obvious you *have* talked about the idea," Pendrax said. He looked quite pleased with himself.

Tar didn't like making long speeches. He especially disliked making long speeches that were ignored.

"Every piss-drunk pirate in Zanz talks about raiding the barges," Tar said. "They also talk about the time they fucked a mermaid. It's nothing *but* talk. Put it out of your mind. Krait has infected you with her love of treasure."

Now Pendrax chuckled.

"I'm a doctor, not a pirate. Treasure means nothing to me."

Tar passed him the jar, signaling an end to the topic. They watched a pod of black-and-white seawolves cruise alongside the Barracuda, then dive out of sight when they saw she wasn't a fishing boat with nets to be stripped of catch. The cetacean equivalent to pirates, Tar mused.

Pendrax broke the silence. He had decided to give it one more try.

"I wouldn't have mentioned the barges at all, except when I left Okré's court, there was talk of a treasure of inestimable value being shipped to Atlantis aboard the barge Gyraf. It's supposed to be a huge secret, but you know what they say in court."

"No, I don't."

"A secret is not a secret until it's told."

That sounded like nonsense to Tar.

"Healer, all that court intrigue has softened your head. It's no secret there's treasure aboard a treasure barge. That's why they're called treasure barges—because they're barges with treasure in them. *It's in the name.*"

Pendrax passed the biridi back, stood, and stretched.

"As I said, it makes no difference to me," he said. "I thought a treasure beyond price was something you'd find interesting, that's all."

Tar went to the rail. He felt he should put the subject of treasure barges to rest—if only so he could urinate in peace.

"According to the ballads they sing in Atlantis," he said, "the only treasure beyond price is true love. So even if we somehow managed to raid this Gyraf of yours, what would we find in the vault? A bonny wench with a big pair of tits."

Pendrax saw his chance.

"If you want to put a specific value on it, I'm told this particular treasure is worth as much as the entire nation of Okré. And they say a lone man could carry it in his hands."

The healer strolled away laughing, as if it meant nothing to him. But in truth he was frustrated.

He had been sure his bait would be irresistible, but it

seemed Tar Yunkai was unique among freebooters. Of all the tens of thousands of pirates that haunted the watery fringes of Atlantis, he was the only one who didn't give a damn about wealth. This was a problem. Pendrax's entire mission hinged on convincing the commanders of the Barracuda to raid that barge.

KRAIT APPEARED at Tar's side while he was relieving himself.

"Checking the depth?"

"The water's too cold," he said.

She punched his arm.

"By the tentacles of Lohaka, did you just make a joke?"

He changed the subject.

"I have an idea. If we run the Cormorant behind the Barracuda like a pursuit, the other warship will think we—"

Krait wasn't listening.

"Were you and that fucking healer arguing just now? That seems like a good reason for me to kill him."

"It wasn't about anything important. He heard some rumor back in Okré about a treasure barge with priceless cargo, and I explained why we don't attack them."

Even as he spoke, Tar wished he hadn't.

"What rumor is this?" Krait asked, sweetly.

8

———

At last, the masters of the ship came to blows.

The crew had been placing bets on the matter since the Barracuda left Zanz, and tonight it seemed that money would change hands.

They fought by moonlight until they smashed a cresset lamp, and then they fought by firelight, heedless of the burning deck.

She came at him with sword and knife flashing like the wings of a flying fish and drove him back across the deck. Then he found an opening and nearly cut off her feet with his boarding-axe. She was forced to retreat as he launched a barrage of furious swings, almost faster than the eye could see.

"Priceless is what we *want*, you maggoty fistula!" she shouted.

With one blow he tore a chunk out of the mainmast, and with another split a burning deck plank in half. The axe caught fire.

"A treasure that costs your life is no treasure at all!" he replied.

As he tore the flaming blade free, she took a chance and nearly stabbed him through the head, but only split his cheek. He brought the axe up so fast it set fire to the slit it made in her ribs. Neither of them was able to land a decisive stroke. The outcome would be determined by who bled to death first.

"I didn't take you for a coward," she snarled.

Krait threw her dagger. Only Tar could have dodged it. The sailor behind him got his foreskin pinned to the gunwale.

"I didn't take you for a fool," Tar replied.

He threw his axe. It clove the air like a whirling firework, nicked the tip of Krait's ear, and buried itself in the figurehead at the prow. She threw her cutlass aside.

The enraged combatants closed with their bare hands, snarling and panting. Krait struck like a tornado made of hands, feet, knees, and elbows, but Tar kept coming as if the bone-crunching impacts were drops of rain. He grabbed her by the crotch and launched her straight up into the air.

She came down on her head, shook it off, and came at him again. She wanted revenge for the groin-busting she'd gotten. She tried to land a long-shot kick to his balls. He caught her foot and threw her into the ocean by her own momentum.

Some sailors ran around stomping out the fires. Others remained where they were in open-mouthed shock. Krait was invincible, yet she had been defeated.

"Seems we have a new captain," Skraj said to Tar. "You're the skipper now."

The First Mate didn't sound very pleased. He'd bet heavily on Krait to win, and was now broke.

Tar spat a long stream of blood on the deck.

"I'm no captain," he said. "Bring the ship about. Get her back aboard."

9

Morning found Tar and Krait kneeling side-by-side on the deck, studying a crude drawing of a treasure barge's internal layout. Pendrax and Hutto the Bee knelt with them.

Hutto had used a burnt stick to scratch the plan onto a piece of canvas. He'd sailed on treasure ships before he took up piracy, and knew a great deal about their construction. He didn't know how to write, so he couldn't label the drawing. Tar wasn't bothered by this, as he couldn't read.

"Gyraf and the rest, they're all built the same," he said. "Five decks. Vaults are in the hold, below the waterline. Loading hatches here and here. You've got your crew quarters here, then armory, kitchen... "

Hutto went on to explain how the ships were built to be unsinkable: the copper-plated outer hull surrounded an inner hull, both of them crafted of thick timber and Atlantean steel. For stability when the barge wasn't heavily laden, the void between the hulls could be filled with ballast stones. Not even a trireme at ramming speed could hope to pierce such a carcass.

Hutto indicated the deck positions of the harpoon cross-bows, which could punch through the Barracuda as easily as they'd transfix a whale. No angle of approach was safe from these. If anyone got past the escort of Triremes, they'd have to scale more than thirty feet straight up the barge's smooth copper hull, while sharpshooters hurled down arrows and harpoons from all directions.

With every new detail Hutto described, it became clearer why nobody had ever attempted to rob one of the barges: it couldn't be done.

"As for getting inside," Hutto continued, "There's cargo shafts, where they lower the vaults in by big-arse cranes. The vaults sit at the very bottom of the hold. They're made of plate iron thick as your fist. I only saw inside the hold once. The vaults looked like strongboxes, big as houses. They rent them to whoever's shipping goods."

"I told you," Tar said to Krait. "It doesn't matter if the treasure is worth all of Okré, or all of the world. We're not getting in."

Krait was in a black mood since they'd fished her out of the sea the previous night.

"In that case, what the fuck was the point of beating your ass?"

She flicked Tar on the ear with her finger. It hurt.

"The next time I throw you overboard, you'll be lashed to an anchor," he warned.

Pendrax saw their tempers rising, and smoothly intervened.

"Hutto, how long has it been since you sailed aboard one of the barges?"

"Nigh on both hands of years, Healer."

"The thing is, I'm told they've been recently fitted with an interesting new feature. Are any of you familiar with a moon pool?"

Nobody knew what he was talking about. Pendrax took up the charcoal and drew an accurate elevation of the design.

"It's a shaft that goes straight down through the bottom of the hull and into the sea. Open at the top. There's a steep staircase down the shaft. You can dive underwater, come back up, and never see the sky."

"I thought Tar was the stupidest pecker-wart in all creation, but I was wrong," Krait said. "You just took the crown."

Pendrax looked around at the others. He'd assumed explaining moon pools would be the easy part, but already Krait was reaching for her dagger.

"None of you pays attention to innovations in marine construction?"

"I watched them make a rowboat in Zanz," Tar offered.

"My guy," Krait said to the healer, "you just made a drawing of a ship with a hole under the fucking waterline. A ship with a hole under the fucking waterline will fucking sink. It's the first thing you learn in sailor school."

"That's what this shaft is for. It extends up *above* the maximum waterline. As far as the barge is concerned, it's the same as if there were no hole at all."

"Hutto," Krait said, "fetch me a cleaver. I'm killing this asshole for wasting my time. Any objections?"

She looked pointedly at Tar.

"Will I forfeit my half of the ship?"

"If you let me kill him, we'll forget that conversation ever happened."

"Let me know when you're available to discuss blockading Khatha's port," he said, and walked away.

Tar didn't like indiscriminate killing, but the healer's death would no longer be indiscriminate. He had made himself a problem one too many times.

. . .

To distract himself from what might be a long, drawn-out series of death screams, Tar went forward to watch some sailors at work. They were fishing over the bow, floating some kind of trap at the end of a rope.

It was a shallow, ring-shaped tub with a tube in the center, open to the water below. Suspended above the tube was a chunk of meat. Tiny bright minnows leaped up at the bait through the tube, overshot, and fell into the tub. Dozens of them were squirming there.

"What is that thing?" he asked.

"Peffering tub," said Lub-Amax, the female sailor who had been shot through the elbow.

She seemed to think this was sufficient information, but Tar stared at her, so she elaborated.

"Those are peffs. Swallow them live and you get high. They can live in the tub for days."

An alarm bell was ringing in Tar's mind.

"Krait! Don't do it!"

The peffering tub now floated in the large basin used to oil sails. The tiny fish had been decanted into a bucket, and the basin was filled with seawater.

Krait glared down with her arms crossed. Her eyes were red with hate. Scraj held Pendrax's neck against the edge of the basin, cleaver in his free hand. Krait had only been persuaded to delay the execution until Tar's demonstration failed.

Much of the crew gathered around, wondering what new madness the Yunkai had in mind.

"Pretend this ring is a treasure barge," Tar said. "The top edge is the deck. The hole in the middle is the moon pool. Look."

He pushed the peffering tub deeper into the basin. The

water rose up inside the ring, the same as it did around the outside of the tub. No water got in.

"You see? It works. He doesn't lie."

"Fuck you," Krait said. "A treasure barge isn't a peffering tub."

"It's the same principle! As long as the walls around the moon pool go up higher than the waterline, it works."

"Fine, It fucking works. But if it fucking works, then why the hell doesn't *every* fucking ship have one?"

Tar scratched his chin.

"For that matter, why does *any* ship have one?"

"Skraj," Krait growled, "Why the fuck would a ship have a fucking moon pool?"

Skraj got down close to Pendrax.

"Why the fuck would a ship—"

"I heard," Pendrax croaked. "Can I stand? I'm choking."

Skraj squinted up at Krait. "Can he stand?"

She kicked Pendrax in the backside. He stood, and spoke only to Tar.

"You're interested in what goes on at court. There's so much treachery these days, none of the powerful in Atlantis want anyone to know what they're doing or where they are."

"Skip the stories," Tar said. "Why would treasure barges have moon pools? You have as long as it takes me to breathe three times."

Pendrax was truly alone. He swallowed hard. What he said next would decide if he ever spoke again.

"The barges dock at specially-built harbors. There are dry, underwater tunnels beneath. They can extend them up to the moon pools. The king, queen, high priests, and so on take these tunnels in and out of the barges. That way, nobody knows who's aboard."

"Why the fuck does that matter?" Krait complained. But he had her attention.

"Did you know," Pendrax said, "the king himself is leading the Atlantean fleet these days? It's true. Apparently, Admiral Sea-Eagle died in a hunting accident."

Of this, they were aware. Unbeknownst to the doctor, it was Tar himself who had disemboweled the admiral.

Pendrax hurried on: "What would happen if assassins knew which ship he was aboard?"

"That's a good fucking point," Krait said. "Can you imagine if we... "

Tar was skeptical. Pendrax didn't lie in obvious ways, but he never told the whole truth.

"Are there moon pools on any warships?" he asked.

"That I cannot say," Pendrax said. "I know only of the treasure barges."

Tar and Krait looked at each other. Neither of them knew what to do next. If what Pendrax said was true, there *was* a way to raid the Gyraf, and the thought was irresistible. But he also had a very good reason to lie—it could delay his execution.

"Tell us more," Tar said.

10

———————

"It's clear this was his plan all along," Tar said. "All that nonsense about stowing away on the first ship he saw, the library in Atlantis and the rest—lies. From the beginning, he wanted us to steal that treasure."

He and Krait stood amidships in the shade of the mainsail. Pendrax had been thrown into the hold until they decided how to proceed.

"But he hasn't mentioned wanting a cut of the fucking profits," Krait said. "So we have to assume he wants us dead. Remember, there are some damn big bounties on our heads."

"I think it's the treasure he wants, but he doesn't want it for himself. My best guess is it belongs to his enemies, and he'll be happy just to know they lost it."

Krait perked up.

"That's a good theory! I'll peel the skin off his fingers until he confirms it."

She drew her dagger.

"Let's not get ahead of ourselves. No matter what, we have to make some big assumptions. First, that the treasure exists. Next, that it's worth as much as he says it is. Then we have to assume it can be carried by one man. What kind of treasure would that be?"

"Not precious metals. Too heavy. It could be a water-clear emerald the size of a fucking pumpkin."

"Or could it be documents?" Tar mused. "The property deed to the king's palace in Atlantis, or something like that?"

He only vaguely understood what these things were, but he knew they were valuable.

Krait punched the palm of her hand.

"Seems like we can agree it's *possible* the fucking treasure is real, priceless, and portable. Yeah?"

"It's possible. But it's more likely he made it up. That leads me back to *why* he wants us to do this. There's a reason he dangled this bait in front of us, and it's something personal. It's not money."

"If he plans to get us killed, there are much easier ways to do it. If we're slaughtered raiding the Gyraf, he won't get the credit or the reward. Our crew will hack him to pieces before they die."

Tar massaged his temples with his fists.

"We're chasing our tails. It comes down to this: we rob the barge, or we don't rob the barge."

"How the fuck would we pull it off? That's a kind of important question as well."

"Concerning that, I have an idea."

It didn't look much like a dolphin on the deck, but once it was in the water, the thing might pass.

There weren't a great many materials aboard the Barracuda suitable for Tar's project, but eventually a crude frame had been made out of heavy rope—a series of loops tied together to form a skeletal tube that tapered at both ends, twice the length of a man.

Then the sailors formed an ill-smelling sewing circle and stitched canvas into a covering for the frame. Now it looked like an outsized yam, or as Krait observed, a giant turd.

Finally, fins carved from oar blades were attached to sides, back, and tail end, and the whole thing was tarred black. It was naturally buoyant, so when they tossed it overboard, tethered to a line, it rode the water much like a dolphin would—and even appeared to flick its tail in the swells. But it did look more like a giant turd than a living animal.

The seas teemed with life in those days, so within minutes, real dolphins had gathered to examine this curious artifact. It must have amused them, for they cavorted and leaped around it. This lent it the illusion of life it had been missing.

The dolphins didn't seem to be bothered by the two human beings who rode head-and-shoulders inside it, their legs trailing beneath.

"It works," Krait said, when she and Tar were hauled up over the rail after the artificial dolphin. "The fucking thing works."

"How did it look?" Tar wanted to know.

"Stupid, until the real 'uns came along," said Lub-Amax. "Then it like blended in."

"If we chop up a sack of peffs, we can get the real ones whenever we want," Krait said. "They love getting fucked up as much as we do."

The two-vessel fleet got underway again, this time angling toward the shipping lane used by the treasure barges. The Barracuda remained on the blind side of the Cormorant, and eventually had to fall back, as naval ships didn't keep company with civilians.

If the Barracuda got too close to one of the other ships, the naval harpoons would respond, so temporary commander Skraj directed her crew to lay off around a mile and a half distant and sail parallel to the Gyraf. Many civilian vessels traveled in the same manner, hoping to enjoy the protection that came from proximity to Atlantis's fleet.

Tar persuaded half of the Cormorant's crew to dress up as Atlantean soldiers, and Krait ordered the square sail trimmed in the naval manner. There could be no visible sign that the ship was under pirate control.

The Cormorant's galley rowers, now that they were getting paid for their work, pulled lustily on their oars. By sunset, the sails of the barges and their escorts pricked the horizon.

They waited until full darkness before joining the convoy that cruised slowly along the shipping lane. Warships often deviated from their courses to check out threats on the sea, coming and going. No lookout in the fleet would think twice about the Cormorant's arrival, as long as she behaved like a warship.

Nobody sang or talked. Only the required running lamps were lit. The Cormorant joined her naval sisters without incident. No flares went up, no alarms were sounded. She was like any of the other Atlantean biremes on the line, sailing through the night.

"Tonight's our chance," Krait said to Tar.

They stood at the Cormorant's rail. The darkness was so thick that only she with her owl's eyes could see the ships around them. Aft was the trireme that sailed ahead of the Gyraf, then the Gyraf itself, flanked by two more triremes, the last trireme out of view behind her. At a distance forward of the Cormorant was an identical bireme to herself, then another barge with its escort of triremes some leagues ahead.

"We haven't properly prepared," Tar said. "Let's stay in the convoy tomorrow and make sure this will work. We can strike tomorrow night. One mistake and we're done."

"It *has* to be tonight, you fucking pussy. There's no moon. It's overcast, too. Not even starlight."

He silently cursed his unhelpful Gods and punched the rail with his fist.

"Assassin's Eve," he said. "Darkest night of the month."

"That's right. My people consider it their lucky time."

"Let's run over it again," he said, and continued:

"We drift back in the dolphin, straight past the leading trireme, then alongside the barge. If there *is* a moon pool, we dive and get aboard. If not, we cut the dolphin's rope and drift, and Barracuda picks us up tomorrow."

Krait took up her favorite part:

"But say we get aboard. Then we kill everybody we fucking meet until we find the dipshit with the keys. We kill him too, and unlock every fucking door until we get to the vault."

Tar concluded:

"We unlock the vault, steal the pumpkin, get back to the moon pool, get back in the dolphin, pull on the signal cord, and the crew hauls us back to the Cormorant. Anything we missed?"

"Like it matters? You know that fucking healer is lying about the moon pool. We're on a suicide mission."

11

They could hear the oars of the trireme hitting the water as they passed close beside it.

All was darkness, so Tar and Krait hung suspended inside the fake animal like the dead in limbo, and drifted ever closer to the barge. It was unlikely anyone could see it at all, the night was so dark.

Their world was a stale pocket of air; they couldn't see each other an arm's length apart. Even Krait's powerful eyes needed at least a *hint* of light. There was none inside the dolphin.

The Cormorant was at the absolute minimum regulation distance from the trireme behind it, yet the journey to the Gyraf was still nearly six hundred feet. The warship's sounding rope had been spliced and spliced again with every spare length of cordage aboard to achieve that length.

At the rope's end, the dolphin came alongside the barge. There was no need to attract living dolphins. It was darkness within darkness.

As it turned out, Pendrax was right about the moon pools.

Tar and Krait left the shelter of the dolphin and dived beneath the massive, flat bottom of the treasure barge. A shaft of yellow light shone straight down through the gloom, its top edge crisply drawn. They swam for it, the hull pressing downa like a thundercloud, blotting out the world above the water.

By the time they reached the source of the light, Tar's lungs were screaming for air. He followed Krait's kicking feet into the glowing square above, surfaced in a well-lit shaft that rose into the ship, and gasped as quietly as he could for air.

They were inside the Gyraf.

A steep, narrow stairway wound around the shaft that ascended from the water. It was almost a ladder, but there was a velvet rope to cling to. The interior of the shaft was richly carved and decorated, which supported the idea that important people used it. The light was strong, thrown from lamps in the chamber above the shaft onto a polished, golden dome ceiling, which reflected down the stairs. It was the source of the glow they'd seen underwater.

Tar carried only a hatchet, Krait only a dagger. They could collect more weapons as they killed their way through the Gyraf.

They reached the top of the stairs and cautiously surveyed the room above the moon pool.

It was a simple box, except for the domed ceiling. The shaft emerged from the center of the floor like the top of a square well, with steps down on each side. The room was furnished with a few upholstered benches and large, ornate oil lamps on tripods. Mildew-speckled tapestries hung on three walls. Into the fourth wall was set a massive door.

They let the water run off them for a few moments, listening. Distant sounds of activity reached their ears, but there was no sound on the other side of the door.

"Shouldn't there be guards here?" Tar whispered.

"It's a fucking trap," Krait said. "I bet there's fifty burly, spear-carrying motherfuckers on the other side of that door."

"Only one way to find out."

Krait took position beside the door. It bore an enormous Atlantean steel lock, but the latch moved freely. Tar eased the door open.

There was a narrow passage on the other side, its walls

and ceiling decorated with tile mosaics in aquatic motifs. At the end was another door.

"If that one isn't locked either, this is definitely a trap," Tar said.

"Despite myself, I agree. If it's open, we go straight the fuck back to the dolphin."

"Deal."

He tried the latch. The door was unlocked. They made eye contact.

"It's open," he said.

They went on through into the next compartment.

And the next, and the next.

Whenever they found a space with multiple doors, all were locked except one. So it was they were lured deeper and deeper into the Gyraf, along a deliberate path. Everywhere they went, they could hear voices and activity. But it was always somewhere else.

"It's going to suck having to die with you," Krait said.

"I'll die last so I can see you go," Tar said.

He checked another door. It opened onto a companionway with stairs leading downward.

"This should lead to the hold," he said.

The ornamental finishes told them where the rich and powerful spent their time. For the last three decks the walls and furnishings had been plain and sturdy, the sort of things expected in a utilitarian craft such as the Gyraf. Down below the waterline, all the riches were in the vaults, not sparkling on the walls.

At the bottom of the stairs was a barred gate. It stood ajar. They slipped through and into a cavernous space. This was the hold. The metal framework of the ship looked like the skeleton of some long-dead whale, extending from back to front of the barge.

Darkness swallowed the details of the hold. A few

lanterns set in brackets revealed brutally heavy construction in metal and timber, coiled heaps of winch chains, and pools of dampness on the floor. Overall, the impression was of a prison cell fit for a dragon.

There was only one vault in the hold. Entirely built of iron, with huge rings on the top and an armored door on the nearest side, it resembled a rust-stained tomb.

"This is it," Tar said. "They must be waiting for us here."

"You blind-ass dunce, there's nobody down here. Those shadows are empty."

"You want to bet the vault door is open, too?"

"I'll bet you your share of the treasure," Krait said.

"It was a figure of speech. I'm not betting anything. If they're coming for us, it will be from behind. I'll keep watch here. Go see if it's open."

He stood out of sight next to the gate at the bottom of the stairs. Krait moved fluidly and silently across the deck of the hold. She seemed more like a shadow come to life than a woman. She may have been banished from her tribe, but she possessed its skills.

The latch clicked as lightly as a dry mouth, and Krait eased the door ajar. Its well-oiled hinges made no sound. Lamplight spilled through the gap. She put her eye to the opening. A gentle voice drifted out of the room.

> He gave to me a silver bird
> That sang so plaintively
> As sweet a song as I have heard
> But I must set it free.
> He gave to me a golden bird
> That spoke as you or I
> It knew the scriptures, every word

But I must let it fly.

Krait threw a glance at Tar. He left his post at the stairs and took position alongside her, hatchet ready. She raised her dagger and threw the door open.

THE VAULT HAD BEEN FURNISHED as a luxurious bed-chamber. Seated upon the drapery-hung bed was a beautiful young woman, richly clothed. She was bending forward to throw dice. Thin, jeweled braids swung about her face.

On a cushion at her feet reclined another well-favored young woman, simply coiffed and plainly dressed. They both looked up with shock when Tar and Krait stepped into the room. The dice rattled to the floor.

"Three red and two blue," Krait said. "Six."

12

———

The two women stayed very still. Tar could taste their fear in the air. He closed the vault door behind him.

The woman on the bed sat up very straight and folded her hands in her lap. It was she who had been singing. Her voice quivered, but she kept it level.

"It is me you have come to kill. Spare my dear maid Chelim."

Krait was too surprised to speak, so Tar made an attempt.

"Were you *expecting* someone to kill you?"

"Why else would you be here?"

"We came to steal a treasure," he said.

He couldn't believe he had to state the obvious, but then, he couldn't believe the vault had women in it. The heist was going sideways at incredible speed.

"Point of order," Krait said. "Regardless of our intentions, if either of you fucking screams, I *will* kill you."

"For whom would we scream?" the woman asked.

"That's a good point," Tar said to Krait. "We didn't see a single guard on the way down here."

Chelim the maid raised her hand.

"I did try to scream when you arrived, but no sound came out."

The woman on the bed addressed her maid:

"You won't scream now, though, will you?"

"No, the moment has passed. Can I have some water?"

A silver pitcher and cups stood on a table by the door, so Tar poured, then handed a cup to Chelim.

"What the fuck are you doing?" Krait said to him.

"She wanted some water."

"By the fucking Gods."

She turned on the women and brandished her dagger.

"No more bullshit. According to our information, there is a priceless fucking treasure aboard this fucking barge, in this fucking hold, in this fucking vault. So here we are. Instead, there's no treasure, priceless or otherwise. Fuck."

"Maybe these curtains are valuable?" Tar suggested.

Krait dragged her hand down her face, straining to master her temper.

"I'm going to check the perimeter," she decided. "There's some heavy-duty fuckery going on here and we are at the center of it."

She opened the vault door and went out.

Tar, having nothing to say, fiddled nervously with his hatchet. He looked the women over to see what he could learn about them.

They were ordinary enough at a glance: hair in braids, naked-breasted, with gauzy, billowing sleeves on their arms, and stiff pleated skirts from hip to ankle.

Chelim, the one on the floor, didn't wear the string of a slave over her shoulder. Therefore she was a free servant. She was nicely plump, with dark, vulnerable eyes. He turned his attention to her mistress.

She was something of a work of art. With the luminous

brown skin, dark lips, and black eyes of the ethnic Atlantean, she would have been born on the island of Atlantis. But she didn't live there, because she was coiffed and dressed in a provincial style. That meant she was from an important family in one of the mainland colonies.

More than that, he could not guess.

"How many months along are you?" he asked the mistress.

"*What?*" gasped Chelim. She clapped both hands over her mouth, scandalized. The other woman merely raised an eyebrow—but so haughtily, it felt like a scolding.

As usual, Tar wished he hadn't said anything.

But the fact was, nearly all the colonial Atlantean women he'd seen attending the fights were heavily pregnant. His now-dead master Heptumu had once explained the phenomenon to him.

None but an island-born Atlantean was permitted to own significant property in its mainland colonies. Therefore, pregnant Atlantean women always came to the island to birth their babies. Otherwise, their children would not be eligible to inherit the family's farms, mines, hunting grounds, or plantations.

At any time, there were thousands of these great-bellied provincial women visiting Atlantis. They were often appallingly rich, and of consequence appallingly bored. Waiting for their babies to come piled tedium on top of tedium. So in order to pass the time, they would attend public entertainments. Of all these, the one show a pregnant woman in Atlantis could not miss was the bloodshed in the Crimson Arena, where Tar had fought.

Atlanteans were highly superstitious. According to an old wive's tale, pregnant women would reliably go into labor within a day of seeing a fight in that arena. As stupid as it sounded to Tar, hundreds of these women (along with their children, siblings, aunties, servants, and slaves) would fill the middling seats at best-seat prices, every day of the week.

How many infants had Tar lured out of their mother's bellies during the course of his fighting career? He shook off the thought, and was surprised to see Krait had returned and was standing next to him, snapping her fingers.

"Did you hear a single fucking word I said?"

"No. I was wondering why she isn't pregnant. Did you see anyone outside?"

"You are one weird motherfucker."

"Until now," the mistress said, "we've always been alone between supper and breakfast. No one visits at night."

Tar turned to Krait.

"So what were you saying before?"

"I was saying this fancy bitch here could be worth some money if we demand a ransom."

"What is a ransom?"

"You can't be fucking serious. We take her away, cut her finger off, and send it to her family. They pay us a lot of money, which is the ransom. Then we tell them where to find her. They come to get her, and we rob them again."

"That sounds awful. Excuse us," he said to the women. "Krait, let's leave."

She caught him roughly by the arm.

"We can't go empty-handed, for fuck's sake," she hissed.

He turned to the two women.

"Maybe you can help. I mentioned we're here for treasure. Have you seen any? It should be here in the hold."

"Who told you of this treasure?" the mistress asked.

"A man I'm going to kill in such a terrible way that it haunts the nightmares of the living for a thousand fucking years," Krait said.

"He's a doctor from Okré," Tar elaborated.

"Okré," the mistress said, thoughtfully.

Tar was mystified by her. She might be any idle, rich daughter of Atlantis—but comported herself with the self-possession of a queen.

She spoke again:

"If I may ask, what did he tell you the treasure is worth?"

"He said it was fucking priceless," Krait said. "But honestly I'd have been happy with anything worth the weight in gold of a bull buffalo."

The woman tapped her finger on her chin. Then she said:

"I'll offer you that much gold to take me back to Okré."

"You're *from* Okré?" Tar asked.

The gold didn't interest him, but the woman did.

"I am. And it's vital that I return."

"Sounds good," Krait said. "But we only work for cash. Unless you can pull that much gold out of your hoo-ha, it's not happening. Tar, you were right for once. This is a setup. Let's get the fuck out of here."

"Wait," said the Atlantean woman. "We must not part as strangers. Who are you?"

The command in her voice indicated that she was accustomed to being obeyed.

Krait struck her most dangerous and sexy pose, the one she used when seducing landlubbers.

"I am Krait Venom, captain of the Barracuda, swiftest hunting boat on the Main. My companion is known far and wide as...the Rectal Destroyer."

Tar pinched the bridge of his nose as if to ward off a headache. He had endured enough of Krait's nonsense for a lifetime.

"My name is Tar Yunkai of Men," he said. "Who are you?"

The woman rose to her feet. Although petite, she seemed to fill the room with her presence. She indicated her servant.

"This is Chelim Okré of Men."

Then she pressed her palms together, opened her hands

wide, and bowed very slightly. It was a gesture of greeting Tar had not seen before.

"And I am Abeka Calyp-Ash," she continued, "Blood of the First King, sole heir of House Wetë."

Krait's eyebrows went halfway up her forehead and her narrow eyes went round. Her jaw fell. She dropped her dagger. It stuck point-first in the parquet floor.

She sank to one knee and bowed in the Atlantean fashion, right arm bent across her back, left hand over her heart.

Tar was mystified. "Who?"

"Royal Princess of all Atlantis," Krait said, "I live and die at your command."

13

———

"I still don't understand," Tar said.

Krait stood up again, considerably less cocky.

"We are in the presence of the future queen of Atlantis."

Tar shrugged. "So?"

There was a furtive sound from outside the vault. The door was ajar; otherwise they would not have heard it. The thieves instantly went on guard, prepared to fight for their lives. Discovery was inevitable now.

"I'll check," Krait said. "Be ready to make a stand."

She plucked her dagger from the floorboards, eased the door open, and slipped into the gloom beyond. Tar closed the door behind her and listened. There wasn't another sound.

The Princess and her maid were backed against the far wall, holding hands. They were putting a brave face on mortal fear. Tar felt he should distract them.

"It's a miracle," he said. "I've never seen Krait treat anyone with respect before."

"What is her tribe?" the princess asked.

"Libagoro of Men."

"Ah."

"As Krait will tell you, I'm an idiot. Can you explain what this means?"

"The Libagoro are neighbors of Okré. Their territory is across the northern border."

"Even so, she bends her knee for no one."

"There's a fuckload more to it than that," Krait said, slipping back into the vault.

She was spattered with blood, her dagger arm red from elbow to blade. As she spoke, she tore down a silken wall hanging and used it to wipe off the blood.

"Are we surrounded?" Tar asked.

"Fuck no. It was only a couple of assassins. Now I know why she thought we came to kill her, anyway. Darkest night of the month."

Chelim nearly fainted. Princess Abeka's face went gray.

"Assassins?"

Krait shrugged. "They weren't Libagoro, so it was hardly a fight. Nobody from my tribe would ever kill the Daughter of House Wetë."

Tar went to the door and looked out. Other than a hand of masked, black-cloaked corpses strewn around the entrance, the hold was empty.

"Princess Abeka," he said, "We'd help you if we could, but it's impossible. There's a moon pool, a long swim, and then we have this fake dolphin—"

"You sound like an insane person," Krait said.

He ignored her. "Regardless, we are *not* kidnapping the first princess of Atlantis. Do you understand who would come after us?"

Krait answered for him.

"Every ship in the empire and all its fucking colonies."

"That is not worth a gold buffalo," Tar said. "We would be —Krait, what's a large number?'

"Ten thousand, three hundred and fifty-one."

"We would be pursued by that many ships."

"Your Highness," Krait said, "it pains me to admit he's right. No sum of gold is worth making an enemy of the entire world."

"Perhaps you misunderstood me," Abeka said. "I meant the weight of a bull buffalo in gold—*each*."

Krait had lost the ability to form words, but Tar wasn't moved.

"Forgive me, Princess. I was a pit-slave until half a year ago. There's more to do before I die. Gold is meaningless to me."

"Your Highness, " Krait said. "I need to discuss business with my partner."

She turned her back to the women, pulled Tar close by his ear, and whispered at the top of her lungs:

"Use your head! According to law, we get to choose the animal. I know where we can get a buffalo the size of—"

"Forget it," Tar said. "Gold is only a metal."

"It's a *magic* metal. Gold transforms into anything you desire."

"I desire freedom, which I already have."

Krait was visibly sweating. Now she spoke in a genuine, low whisper:

"Look, when you told her we wouldn't do it, I assumed it was a negotiating tactic. And it worked. You doubled the fucking price. But you weren't negotiating, were you?"

"No. We can't outrun every ship in the world."

Krait stepped back, chin up, the picture of defiance.

"The Barracuda can."

Tar saw the promise of gold had driven her mad. It was up to him to save their lives, and they were out of time. He turned to Abeka:

"What you ask is impossible, and what you promise is impossible. Nobody has tons of gold at their disposal."

Krait slapped her forehead.

"Okré's where the gold *comes* from, man!"

Tar turned on Krait and shook her shoulders.

"By the Nameless Gods, woman, *think*! She may be a princess, but unmarried Atlantean women don't control property. She would have to ask someone for the gold—and tell them what it's for. Then we'd die!"

Abeka laughed despite herself.

"You would be correct were it any woman but me. My uncle Duke Illusan rules Okré, but all of its gold belongs to me."

14

———

Tar could not believe what was happening.

They slipped out of the vault easily enough. He had to carry Chelim past the dead assassins, as she was paralyzed with fear. Yet after that, no new obstacle presented itself. Now and again they heard muted footsteps and voices elsewhere aboard the ship, but none came their way. Within minutes they were back in the chamber above the moon pool.

"Can you swim underwater?" Tar asked his unexpected companions.

"This is a fine fucking time to ask that," Krait observed.

"Yes," Abeka said. "Both of us."

"We're going to be doing some swimming," Tar said. "This is a moon pool—"

"We know," Abeka said. This is where we boarded the ship, by a dry underwater hallway."

"We didn't bring a hallway," he said. "We've got to swim under the Gyraf to our dolphin, which is alongside the hull."

"If the princess drowns, we're fucked," Krait mused out loud.

She was starting to have second thoughts.

"This is a suicide mission," Tar replied. "Your own words."

As if to underline his point, a bell started clanging elsewhere aboard the barge. Then horns blared. Feet hammered the decks.

The door burst open and six armored men charged through it.

Tar leaped at them. His hatchet was lost in the face of the first soldier, so he wrenched the sword from his hand and stabbed the next one in the throat. After that, it was a haze of blood and steel. Chelim's screams out-shrilled the warning bell.

Krait stayed back, dagger up. She was the last line of defense, with Abeka and Chelim behind her, pressed against the wellhead.

More men were coming. Tar drove his shoulder into the last of the six who had gotten through the door. Their combined weight slammed it shut. The soldier was unconscious. Tar let him live.

"Jump!" he shouted to his companions.

He jammed the sword into the gap between door and frame, making a wedge. It would slow their attackers, but not for long.

It was a long drop down the well, but there was no time for climbing the ladder. Iron-nailed sandals were rampaging toward the door.

The princess jumped feet-first, then Chelim. They kicked away underwater so Krait and Tar wouldn't land on their heads.

"Come on, you dickhead," Krait said.

She followed the other women, diving neatly down the shaft.

Tar ran and vaulted himself over the top at the same moment a mass of soldiers began hammering at the door.

15

———

Tar thought Chelim was the slowest swimmer alive. As they swam beneath the hull, he stayed behind her, even as the distance between her and the princess grew. The vast, black bottom of the Gyraf hung over them like a death sentence.

Under the hull, the waves and wind did not trouble them. But the visibility was bad. The women in front of Tar looked like ghosts. He couldn't see Krait at all.

Then the sea lit up around the perimeter of the hull. Soldiers had thrown down waterproof torches.

Tar's lungs were clenching like fists. He felt the pulse beating in his eyes, his flesh demanding he draw breath. Suffocation had begun. His hands and feet, his testicles—cold seawater seemed to have replaced the blood in them.

He kicked with renewed speed, passing beneath the ring of torches. Arrows probed the water near him, trailing strings of pearly bubbles. The archers were shooting blindly. They hit nothing.

Chelim wasn't swimming anymore. She drifted in the water like kelp. Tar surged toward her and caught her hair.

With his remaining hand, he clawed forward through the water.

It was too late. He would have to rise to the surface. He was out of air and his lungs were spasming. The men on the deck of the Gyraf would fire their springbow harpoons, and that would be the end of his short and violent life.

Then, through the fireworks exploding in his vision, he saw the dolphin. Abeka was kicking her way up into its belly. With a final, desperate effort, he closed the distance, each thrash of his limbs less powerful than the last. Even as he felt his skull filling with ice, he came up gasping for life in the dark confines of the dolphin, dragging Chelim up with him.

The servant retched seawater out of her lungs. Tar held her up until she was breathing regularly.

"Good save, monkey-boy," Krait said.

She pulled the cord that would alert the Cormorant to their return.

THE SUN HAD NOT YET RISEN, but the sky was turning pale and the sea had gone from black to deepest indigo.

On the afterdeck, the Princess and her maid huddled together under a rough blanket, shivering and blue-lipped. Pendrax checked their pulses, looked into their ears and eyes, and felt their temperatures with his hand on their foreheads. Tar watched him with suspicion.

"Hear me!" Krait shouted.

"Aye, Skipper!" Replied the crew of the Cormorant. They had gathered the moment the dolphin was hauled alongside.

Increasingly distant, aft of the Cormorant, events were still unfolding aboard the Gyraf. The biremes surrounding it began circling the barge in a defensive formation. Flares lit the water around them, attracting shoals of squid. None of them paid any attention to the Cormorant. She wasn't expected to get involved.

"The good news first," Krait said. "As you can see, we did it. We found the treasure at great peril to ourselves, and brought it back."

The entire crew could not resist a cheer. Krait closed her raised fist for silence.

"The bad news: it's her."

She pointed at Abeka. A gust of chatter rippled through the crew.

"Shut the fuck up," Krait explained. "She going to live, healer?"

"She's half-frozen," Pendrax said. "But otherwise no worse for wear."

Tar scowled at him. The only good untrustworthy man was a dead one. The healer had either lied or been cheerfully misinformed about the nature of the treasure. Either way, the next time Krait wanted to kill him, Tar would not intervene.

Krait was speaking again.

"We got aboard the Gyraf according to plan. Fought our way to the hold. But the vault was empty. Then we ran into her. She has a cubic shitload of loot at home. So there's been a change of plans. We're not hunting for biremes anymore. She hired us to take her back to Okré."

There were many skeptical looks passed around.

First Mate Skraj cocked an eyebrow.

"Pardon me asking, Skipper, but in your estimation, what's a cubic shitload worth in serpents, monetarily speaking?"

"Imagine the biggest fucking bull buffalo you ever saw," she said. "Horns as long as your legs, body like a mountain, and a pair of nuts you couldn't lift with both hands."

Several of the crew closed their eyes, the better to imagine it.

"Now picture this buffalo made of the purest, tenderest Okrean gold—stem to stern. Solid fucking gold. That, my dear comrades, is a cubic shitload."

MINUTES LATER, the Cormorant launched yellow and green flares to indicate her intentions, then dipped out of the convoy to chase off a three-masted felucca that had come too close to the line. This turned into a pursuit.

When the Cormorant didn't return to its place in the morning, they'd assume it was simply elsewhere in the convoy—or still hunting. Patrol ships followed their own courses.

ONCE THE CORMORANT and Barracuda were out of sight of the navy, they hove close together. News was exchanged. Krait relayed the alteration in their plans. As soon as everyone knew what was going on, they set sail toward the mainland.

They'd reach for the nearest point of land first, and then coast to Okré. The Cormorant would have to be abandoned at sea.

Everyone aboard the Barracuda wanted to hear about the night's work in the Gyraf. Krait loved a good story, and she exaggerated how many men they'd killed and the narrowness of their escape. But discretion stood by her that day. She never gave away any hint of Abeka's true identity. Their passenger was a rich mainland Atlantean, and that was all.

IT WAS mid-morning under a hot sun before Tar was able to get Krait to himself.

They stood at the aft rail of the Cormorant's top deck. She handed him a skin of biridi. They passed it back and forth.

"Do you not understand the danger we're in?" he asked her.

"You think I'm not fucking aware of the enemies we just made? Two groups: whoever wants her dead, and whoever wants her alive. In other words, everybody."

"But you're just laughing and making up rhino-shit stories like there's nothing to worry about. "

"Pretend we won, will you? Because we fucking did. We successfully robbed a treasure barge, which has not happened in decades—many, many hands of years. Enjoy the moment."

He wasn't going to let her put him off.

"You said very few people could have arranged for the princess to be killed. How many is very few?"

Krait raised her hand and counted off her fingers.

"The King and Queen of Atlantis. The King's brothers Illusan and Shadra—one is Duke of Okré, and the other is High Priest. The queen's brother is dead, so he's out. Next best candidate would be the High Admiral, except you split him in half."

"Only a hand of people."

"You got it. Here's the upside: as far as anybody knows, a couple of pirates grabbed the princess, jumped into the sea, and were never seen again. Drowned and gone. Nobody knows we have command of the Cormorant. Nobody knows the Barracuda is involved."

"So we could get her home? It's possible?"

Krait squinted at the horizon.

"We better fucking hope so."

16

The breeze was steady and both ships made excellent headway. With each minute that passed, they drew farther away from the scene of the crime.

Abeka joined them on deck. She was now dressed in dry sailor's clothes—a roughly pleated canvas kilt, a plain sash, and a pair of marlin-skin sleeves. She had bound her braids up in a twist of rope, as sailors did.

She looked like a child in a costume to Tar. He couldn't decide if it was charming or pathetic.

"Feeling better?" he asked her.

"I've never felt better—or smelled worse," she laughed.

Krait was all for the costume. "You look fucking *hot,*" she said, her lust undisguised.

"I see," Abeka said. She was deeply embarrassed.

Tar saw her distress.

"We were talking about the journey ahead," he said. "Krait thinks we're home free, but the hardest part is going to be Okré itself."

Krait snorted.

"There's so much you both don't know," Abeka said. "And so much you *can't* know."

"We should know any-fucking-thing that affects our plans," Krait said. "Drink this."

Abeka took a polite sip of biridi and made a wry face. She looked over the main rail of the Cormorant as if the answer to her dilemma was written on the waves.

"You're pirates. How can I trust you?"

"Then don't," Krait said, and belched loudly.

"There's something you want to tell us," Tar said. "Start with that."

The princess watched a pair of live dolphins race alongside the ship. They seemed to help her decide.

"I don't know who wants me dead," she said. "But I do know who locked me in the hold."

"Ten serpents on her father," Krait said to Tar.

"Duke Illusan, my uncle," Abeka said. "He intends to marry me in Atlantis while my father is away at sea."

"Fuck," Krait said. "Knife in your heart or uncle in your twat. Damn."

It appeared Abeka was freshly realizing how bad her situation was. She took the skin of biridi back and downed an eye-watering swallow.

"My father would never permit such a marriage," she gasped. "But since the admiral died, he's been away from Atlantis, in command of the royal navy. By law, the king can stop royal court marriages from happening, but he can't annul them once they have."

For once, Tar felt he understood what was going on:

"So this uncle smuggles you to Atlantis, marries you, and when your father dies, he gets to rule instead of you."

"Just so."

"That means," he continued, "your uncle put you in the

vault to keep you *alive*. So he's not the one who ordered the assassination."

"What about the queen?" Krait asked.

Abeka seemed seemed relieved to speak her woes, even to buccaneers.

"My mother is too weak to do such a thing. When my father put her twin brother on trial for treason, she never spoke a word against it. She let me be sent to my uncle's court in Okré without any protest at all. She doesn't care if anyone lives or dies."

Krait spat over the side.

"I know how that shit goes," she grunted. "I got disowned by my whole fucking clan. What about your other uncle, the high priest?"

"Shadra is the youngest, so he has risen as far as he ever will—unless his older brothers die. He hates them both."

"It has to be him," Tar said. "Could he order the crew of the Gyraf to look the other way?"

"Any of them could," Abeka said.

"We're back where we fucking started," Krait said. "Stick to the plan. We haul ass for the coast, then hug the shore in the Barracuda. Get to Okré, run up the river to the capitol, collect our gold."

"It's not that easy," Tar said. "We're up to our necks in a royal conspiracy to murder the heir to the throne."

"By the fathomless gash of the Eternal Whore," Krait protested, "Don't worry about the future. The crew will probably kill us in our fucking sleep tonight, and hold her for ransom tomorrow. That's what I'd do."

THE CREW DID NOT KILL them the first night, which meant that Tar kept himself awake for nothing.

Just as the sailors didn't know he was the Golden Prince,

famed butcher of the arena, they did not know that the beautiful mainland Atlantean woman was heir to the entire empire.

In the morning, Tar ordered Pendrax to attend to their guests. They were in the captain's cabin of the stolen warship. He didn't trust the doctor for an instant, but it would heap disaster on disaster if the princess died of a chill.

"They're in excellent health," Pendrax said. "With the proper kit, I could be more thorough, but—"

"I'll follow you out shortly," Tar said.

Pendrax left the cabin. The women were eating the pirate staple of dried fish soaked in wine. Abeka seemed content enough. Chelim was not.

"This must be a rougher life than you're used to," Tar said.

"The food is worse," Abeka replied.

"The beds, the company, the décor and the sanitation are also worse," said the maid.

"I must be the first princess of Atlantis ever to relieve herself over the side of a pirate ship," Abeka laughed.

"Your Highness!" Chelim gasped.

"We're not at court, dear Chelim. This is a different life, and we must live it for a while. Let's not obsess over a temporary loss of comfort. Many would say we've been too comfortable for too long."

"Be careful, both of you," Tar said. "Chelim, never call her 'highness' again aboard ship. She's 'your lady' or 'mistress' for now, nothing more."

"It's force of habit," the maid said.

"Overcome it. Abeka, remember to avoid eye contact with the crew. Remember your role. Krait is the captain here, and you're nobody of importance."

"What do you mean?"

"When you're on deck you look entirely at ease, as if you

own the ship. You stare the sailors down without a thought. You're supposed to be afraid of these people. They're pirates, not gondoliers."

"Chelim is right. It's force of habit. We must do better."

"Thank you," Tar said. He turned to go.

"Tar Yunkai," Abeka said.

She sounded hesitant for the first time.

"Your flesh is marked with battles, but you are soft-spoken and polite. You care nothing for gold, yet fight alongside pirates. May I ask what manner of man you are?"

He considered this. She had no point of reference to understand the life he had led, or the man it had made him. His scars were countless, each one the signature of a dead opponent. Unmarked people like her were the very reason slaves existed.

"The manner of man who pays the price of empire," he said.

17

———

Tar was napping on a coil of rope.

The sailors tried to make less noise around him. If they had once shunned him for freeing the galley slaves, they liked him well enough now. He had invented a new way to capture ships, successfully robbed a treasure barge, and promised them all a fortune. Such a man was difficult to hate.

Later that day, he saw Abeka discreetly weeping at the bow, one arm draped over the carved barracuda figurehead. At the far end of the ship, Chelim's attention was on Krait. The pirate was telling tales of her adventures in an obvious play to get the maid interested in her.

Tar wasn't sure what he should do, but a little conversation might help, if he could think of something to talk about.

"Princess," he said.

She sniffed hard to clear her nose and patted her face dry.

"Yes, Tar Yunkai?"

"Are you troubled that death stalks you?"

"Of course."

In hindsight, he realized it was a stupid question.

"That is why you weep?"

"I weep because I'm helpless. How am I to rule an empire someday, when today I can't even rule my own fear?"

This was a subject he knew well. He quoted his fighting-master:

"Fear is the greatest enemy. It is a trickster that shows us our destruction. We believe it, and are destroyed."

"How do you overcome it?"

"Stare back at fear and it leaves you alone. You'll learn how to do it, and then you'll turn cruel and command the world."

She didn't catch the bitterness in his words—for her, ruthlessness was merely a family trait.

"I command nothing but Chelim," she rued.

LATER IN THE DAY, it was Abeka who approached Tar. He was leaning on the rail, staring at some whales spouting in the distance.

"What are you thinking about?" She asked.

"I was wondering if birds can fly so high they become afraid of heights."

She laughed, not unkindly. "Truly?"

"My thoughts are small," he said.

Without realizing it, she adopted his pose, leaning on the rail.

"What do you think about when you're fighting? Do you think of what moves you're going to make? Do you plan your actions or make strategies?"

"No. I fight until I win. Then I make plans."

"So what's going through your mind as you hew your way through your enemies?"

"Can you read a book and think about something else at the same time?"

"Definitely not."

"Fighting is the same. Thinking is for the past and the future. The past and future have no place in a fight."

FOR SEVERAL DAYS, the two mismatched ships sailed in company. The breeze died off, which was the Barracuda's fatal flaw. She couldn't move in still air. So rowers from the Cormorant volunteered to ply their oars. As there wasn't a full complement of rowers for either vessel, progress was slow. There was time to swim, mend, and drink. Much-needed rest was gotten. Lookouts watched all day and night —the canoes could reach another naval ship at any time.

Chelim and Abeka relaxed into the pirate's life quicker than Tar expected. There were no formalities or social status aboard the ships. The women had no work to do, so their days were idle. The sheer novelty of being around common folk was interesting to them, and they appeared to be trying it on themselves.

He found the women interesting simply because they were strangers, but Abeka became familiar to him quickly, after which he found her interesting on her own merits. They were of similar age, although from the extreme opposites of caste and society. They could not have been more different in that regard—but the difference caught their mutual attention.

The wind picked up in the wee hours of the fifth day since the escape from the Gyraf. That afternoon, the Barracuda parted ways with the Cormorant. It had reached the end of the area of sea it was assigned to patrol. If the warship continued on to the mainland, suspicions would be aroused.

On top of that, the defeated soldiers in their canoes had

plenty of time to reach Atlantis, so any ships coming fresh from there would know the Cormorant was in pirate hands.

Tar and Krait argued furiously for some time as to what must be done, nearly crossed swords, and eventually decided the best course of action was to fire the Cormorant and let her sink.

The Cormorant's volunteer crew rigged the remaining canoes with sail, loaded them with food and water, and accepted as much plunder as the canoes would carry. The seriously wounded were placed aboard.

In three or four days, the sailors would reach land. From there they would easily find work on another ship. They were only pirates while aboard a pirate craft.

"I STILL THINK we should have killed them," Krait said, watching the flames devour the warship.

The canoes were already specks in the distance.

"You can't kill everyone you meet," Tar said.

"I did it for fucking *years*. Never a problem. The one asshole I didn't kill was you, and now everything has gone to shit. I was going to sell that tub for parts."

"You'd lose a fortune in gold to pick up a copper coin from the street," Tar said.

"Frugality is a virtue," Krait said.

She had heard that from someone, and probably killed them for saying it. But it sounded right for this occasion.

A rapid volley of missiles sent everyone to the deck. The rivets that held the bronze plating to the Cormorant's hull had begun to superheat. They peppered the Barracuda and hissed into the sea.

"Get her underway!" Krait shouted.

The Barracuda's three sails filled with wind and her wake turned white as she picked up speed. Soon the Cormorant was out of sight, her position marked by a thick column of gray smoke.

"So now we sail for Okré as fast as we can," Tar said. "Then we have to get to the capitol somehow."

Krait juggled a smoldering rivet off the deck and threw it overboard.

"Do you have a brilliant fucking idea for that leg of the trip?"

"No."

"We should have held out for three buffaloes."

Fut-Ye, a female sailor from Krait's original crew, trotted up to them. She had her hand over her mouth. Blood ran between her fingers.

"Beg pardog, fkipper," she said.

"Bite your tongue?" Tar asked.

She grinned to show them her upper two front teeth were gone.

Took a rivet in fe teef, Chief Tar. I can't find fe healer."

"He's probably below deck," Tar said.

"I looked," Fut-Ye said. "Fearched from ftem to ftern."

"You'll have a fine pair of shiny gold teeth after this," Krait said, and then cupped her hands and bellowed.

"Hear Me!"

"Aye, Skipper!" shouted the crew.

"Find me the fucking sawbones!"

It took only a brief search to determine that Pendrax was not aboard the Barracuda. The news had just been delivered to Krait when the lookout atop the mainmast shouted down:

"Captain! Larboard quarter stern!"

Everyone on deck turned to look. Behind the Barracuda on the left-hand side, nearly at the horizon, was the pillar of smoke rising from the Cormorant. From the heart of it, every color of flares shot into the morning sky, one after another.

Blue, red, green, yellow, purple, white. They arched higher and higher and burned out at their zeniths.

Tar looked at Krait.

"Fly hither to me?"

She spat on the deck.

"I think your precious doctor's been busy," she said. "The chase is on."

18

———

It was a perfect day for sailing. The sea shone like knapped flint. A steady following wind rushed over the chop. Every inch of canvas on the Barracuda was as stiff as sheet iron. The sails were set in a broad reach, nearly kissing the sea. She heeled over so hard the waves raced along the top of her main rail, and only the starboard keel was underwater.

The able sailors joyously sang their songs of disaster and tuned the Barracuda's rigging with the precision of a harp. Every knot of speed she could possibly make had been wrung from the sails.

Still, Krait strode the deck roaring out orders, legs splayed wide against the drunken tilt of the deck. At her command, the crew hurled cargo and spare gear over the sides to lighten the hull. A spar was rigged on the figurehead to bend a headsail to the foremast, then a flying jib to exploit the remaining length of the spar.

The Barracuda was designed for oars and sail, built light and flexible to be driven ashore. With this much canvas above, the hull began to groan. Beads of seawater glistened between the strakes. If the planks parted, she would flood in moments and dive to the bottom like a heron.

Even the masts themselves began to bow, strained to the absolute limits of their strength.

Tar had taken to following Krait as she marched up and down the deck, exhorting the crew to find another fraction of a knot of speed.

"If we sink, we won't get to shore at all," he pointed out.

"Haul in those port backstays until they sing, you poxy bastards!" she shouted. "If that mast cracks, I'll fuck your livers with *his* prick!"

She was referring to Tar, so at least she was aware of his presence. But he couldn't get her attention. At his wit's end, he caught her by the arm and spun her around.

"Krait! By the Gods! You're tearing this ship apart!"

She turned on him, plucking at the hilt of her dagger. Her face was maniacal, the pebbled scars of her tribe encircling eyes as red as wounds.

"Stand down, mainlander. You don't know shit about sailing, and you don't know shit about the Barracuda. I've sailed her this hard in a typhoon."

"Then think of our passenger! You won't get your precious golden buffalo if she dies of sickness."

Abeka and Chelim were curled up in the prow, clinging to the base of the figurehead. They were profoundly seasick, soaking wet from the spray that flew over the bows. Krait glanced at them, indifferent.

"Nobody ever perished of fresh air," she said, and went back to shouting orders.

There was no reasoning with Krait. She was gripped by madness. Tar made his way forward with difficulty—he wasn't accustomed to traversing a deck stood nearly on edge —and knelt in front of the princess and her maid. Chelim was the color of a week-old corpse, and clearly felt like one.

Abeka's dark eyelids and lips were in stark contrast to her pale, greenish face.

"The captain says she'll go easier soon," Tar lied. "It won't be like this too much longer."

Abeka shook her head, which nearly caused her to throw up again.

"Tell her to make all possible speed," she said. "Don't let our discomfort slow us down."

"If we go any faster, the Barracuda might come apart."

"Those flares," Abeka said, swallowing against a wave of nausea. "Every ship my father has will be coming this way."

"Endure this for a while," Tar said. "Once we're on the river in Okré, it's smooth water."

"I don't think we'll be taking the river," she said, but didn't elaborate. She was too ill to speak anymore.

The top of the masts were tipped so low to the water a lookout would see more fish than sky, but one of the sailors working to keep the masts from pulling free had a fine view from the upper main rail.

"Skipper!" he shouted. "Sails ahoy!"

Tar and Krait climbed the deck to the rail and stared at the horizon. As a shark's jaw was crowded with teeth, the entire rim of the world was crowded with sails.

Atlantis was coming for its daughter.

19

———————

For a day the Barracuda ran landward. As there was no more speed to be got from the vessel, Krait had nothing left to do but see who got to shore first. All eyes were on the fleet behind them. A few ships had gotten closer, but none could overtake. Flares were constantly going up as the navy coordinated its actions by the only means it had to communicate.

The sailors would read these aloud, which only made the tension worse.

"Off the stern quarter! That lugger is planning a run at us."

"East nor-east. Looks like a trireme. Says they could cut us off."

Tar's mind was racing. He paced the deck for hours, frequently checking to see that the princess and her maid still lived. Eventually they had recovered enough to move around the ship, which gave him even less to do.

"In the name of the Benthic Cloaca," Krait said to him, "will you settle down, Chief?"

She handed him her skin of biridi.

"I want to fight, not run," he muttered, and drank.

"Not with the princess aboard. I'm not going to be the Libagoro that gets the Daughter of House Wetë killed."

"Explain to me why she, of all the people in the world, is sacred to your tribe?"

This had been bothering Tar since they found the princess in the vault.

"You don't know the story?"

"I don't know *any* stories."

Krait took a long pull of biridi.

"We call it the War Won With a Single Stroke. A few years back, Duke Illusan decided he wanted to take our land from us. He massed ten thousand fucking soldiers on our border. In Libagoro we don't have an army, but we're all assassins, so we sent a small diplomatic mission to his palace."

"To kill him," Tar said.

"Nothing gets past you. They made themselves invisible and reached the throne room, prepared to strike down the duke. The princess was already there, shouting in his face. She was reminding him that our treaty of peace went back unbroken for five generations—a hand. He told her to fuck off. Mind you, she was only like fourteen summers old at the time."

"Thirteen," Abeka said.

She and Chelim had made their way to the place where Tar and Krait stood.

"Your Highness! Have a belt of this," Krait said, and handed her the skin of biridi.

"Anyway," she continued, "her cunt had barely started bleeding, and she was already challenging her uncle's authority! That takes gigantic balls."

"So what happened?" Tar said, cringing at Krait's metaphors almost as much as Chelim.

"She said if her uncle sent even one soldier into Libagoro

territory, she'd cut her own throat, and her pappy, King of Atlantis, would skin him alive. He thought she was bluffing. Laughed at her and called her a foolish child. So—she did it."

"She cut her own... That is, you cut your own throat?" Tar said, switching from Krait to Abeka.

The princess didn't speak, but lifted her jeweled braids and turned her head to show him the side of her neck. There he saw a thin, jagged scar extending from earlobe to jugular.

"But you didn't die," Tar said.

Abeka let her hair fall back.

"Cutting throats is not as easy as it looks."

It absolutely *was* that easy, Tar thought, but it may have been her first time.

"Anyway," Krait continued, "our assassins revealed themselves and saved her life. The duke decided not to invade our land, and we've had peace ever since. We honor Abeka Calyp-Ash, daughter of House Wetë, as we honor very few others."

Tar was amazed to hear this. Why would anyone sacrifice their life for something as abstract as an agreement their great-great-grandfather had made? It made no sense to him.

Abeka shook her head.

"I don't deserve it. To be honest, I was just so angry and frustrated. I thought my father loved me until he sent me away at the age of ten—to be raised by a man I hardly knew. Once I *did* know him, it was worse. My uncle is a monster. I hardly needed a reason to cut my throat."

"Don't be fooled by this bullshit modesty," Krait said. "She may look as weak as a piss-drinking mosquito, but her backbone is made of solid Marean steel."

"She doesn't mean to insult you," Tar said to Abeka.

"It was a *compliment*," Krait snapped.

"Sails ahead," a sailor shouted. "We're surrounded!"

20

The countless flares must have been seen by ships to landward. Another armada was coming at the Barracuda, the sails rising up along the horizon. They were cut off from the mainland. Due north or south were the only clear ways through, and of no use to them. They weren't prepared for the month-long voyage it would take to make land in either of those directions.

"Come about," Krait shouted.

"Skipper," Skraj said, "We can't sail for Atlantis."

"If I tell you to sail up the ass of a leviathan, you haul the sheets! Hard about, sharpish!"

The Barracuda lurched and yawed as the sails were reset and she reversed course. It felt as if the world was spinning. Tar put his arms around Abeka and Chelim to keep them from falling down. They didn't have their sea legs.

"Why are we turning around?" he asked Krait.

"You remember when we decided our plan to raid the Gyraf was so stupid, they wouldn't have thought of it? What's the stupidest thing we could possibly do right now?"

. . .

WITH THE FLEET coming at them, and the Barracuda coming at the fleet, the hours of distance between them turned to minutes. Once-small sails began to bristle up. Soon they could see the oars, the sailors, and the harpoon guns of the warships.

The Barracuda was bearing straight for a monoreme, a single-galley vessel about her size. There were heavy biremes on either side of her.

The faces of the crew and soldiers were clearly visible when a harpoon was launched from its foredeck. One of the Barracuda's sailors was torn off his feet and hurled into the sea, the barbed lance jutting out of him like a mast. They could hear frantic orders to cease fire shouted from the monoreme—the princess could have been killed.

Perhaps this danger was what cracked the warship captain's nerve. He ordered his vessel to break the line of ships as the Barracuda came straight on—so instead of hitting head-to-head, the pirate vessel sheared off all the oars down one flank of the monoreme. The crackle of splintering wood and shouts of panic were behind them in moments, and then the Barracuda was streaking northwest. One of the biremes reversed position by means of its oars, accidentally snapping the bow off the smaller warship. The other bireme circled back to rescue the crew of the sinking vessel.

The charge had worked. Some rigging had been torn out of the Barracuda but she was fully seaworthy. Only one of the three nearest enemy ships was coming after her, and that from a standstill. She was out of harpoon range. There was nothing left to do but run.

IT WAS deep in the night. Tar was at the stern, taking a turn at the tiller to keep the ship on course. Abeka, sleepless, joined him again.

"Are you thinking about anything?"

"Yes."

"What is it?"

"In a society founded on slave labor," he said, "the value of a free man's labor is reduced by the man who labors for free. In that way, poverty is the product of slavery. But the poor cannot rise up to demand what their work is worth, because the penalty for that is to be made a slave. What happens to the gold that isn't paid to slaves or the poor? It enriches the rich. Despite its golden towers and magnificence, this empire is not built on wealth. It's built on poverty."

Abeka stared at him as if he'd sprouted leaves.

"I thought you were going to say something like 'Do fish know they're wet?'"

"That's a good question, too."

They watched the luminous wake of the Barracuda flicker and fade into the darkness behind them. This time, Tar broke the silence.

"I don't think fish know they're wet. We don't have a word for being covered in air, do we? A fish only notices if it gets dry."

She gazed at him.

"You are a philosopher in your own way, Tar Yunkai of Men."

21

In the darkest hour, they sailed into a bank of fog. Tar relinquished the tiller to Skraj—he wasn't sufficiently skilled as a sailor to keep a course in total darkness. The fog erased all sight. Instead, he carried Abeka below decks.

She had fallen asleep, and scarcely stirred when he picked her up. When he placed her beside Chelim, the sleeping maid put a protective arm around the princess, unaware she did so.

Tar looked at them for a few moments. They were lit by a twist of tallow that burned as yellow as a hawk's eye. He felt a strange sense of responsibility for them—especially the princess. In some way, their lives were connected, as if a small part of her now flowed in his veins. He could not define it.

"Island ho!" The lookout cried.

Nobody else could see the pre-dawn Atlantean skyline. The night fog had not dissipated at sea level. But everyone aboard the Barracuda crowded the fore rail to look. Even

Abeka and Chelim stared into the gray blur as if they could will Atlantis into view.

"Hear me!" Krait shouted.

"Aye, Skipper!" replied the crew in unison.

"We'll reach Atlantis in less than two hours. If this fog holds, we can beat the first alarm. Then you're going to do what this asshole says."

Tar stepped into the middle of the deck.

"I'm told you can all swim. Is that true?"

"Slowly," said a sailor.

"On my back," said another.

The rest were confident enough.

"Then swim you shall," Tar said. "There are fishing nets all the way around Atlantis, right at the waterline. One by one, you're going to jump overboard and pull for the nets. They'll support your weight and protect you from predators."

"The sharks and sea wolves and giant jellyfish and what-not?" Skraj asked.

"Don't think about them. Follow the nets to the nearest pontoon. There will be chain ladders there. Keep going upwards and inland and you'll reach the street."

"What then?" asked Lub-Amax.

She was carefully flexing her wounded elbow. It had mostly healed, but wasn't the same as before. She must have been thinking about the swim.

"Then," Tar said, "Nothing. None of this ever happened. You're ordinary sailors in Atlantis, looking for a few drinks and a berth back to the mainland."

"Thoundth good to me," said the sailor who had lost her front teeth.

"One more thing," Tar said. "Never mention anything that happened on this cruise. If you do—"

"You will die," Krait said. "Atlantis hears everything, and it will not fucking spare you. Neither will I."

· · ·

EACH SAILOR WAS GIVEN standard pay for the cruise, with no shares of the treasure, because they couldn't divide Abeka up into two dozen pieces. They tied their gold around their necks in sealskin bags, tucked what little else they owned into their sashes, and waited by the starboard rail.

Atlantis loomed up on the left, its gray-green pontoons rising like weirdly carved cliffs above the fog. The damp chill of the mist and the profound green shadow of the city cast a silence over the Barracuda. None of the watchmen up in the Atlantean defenses could see the pursuing warships yet, so as far as they knew, the Barracuda was nothing more than a sword-fishing boat coming in after a night's hunt.

"Now," Tar said, and the first sailor dived overboard.

HALF THE CREW had gone into the sea and disappeared in the fog before the sky lit up with dancing colors.

"Flares," the lookout called. "They're almost on us."

"Come the fuck down down and swim for it," Krait called back.

The pirate descended the mast and saluted her sailor-fashion with his fist against his brow.

"Been an honor, Skipper," he said, and leaped into the brine.

"We're out of time," Tar said. "Listen, those are the warning horns in Atlantis. The watchmen will be looking for us from here on. The rest of you—all together, get into the water now. Split up before you reach the streets."

"We'll raise a jar to you both," Skraj said.

"Drink to the Golden Prince," Tar replied.

Skraj narrowed his eyes, but there was no time for questions. With a shake of his head, he joined the others over the side and began swimming into the fog.

Now there were only four souls aboard the Barracuda.

"What happens next?" Abeka asked.

Chelim was clinging to her arm with white-knuckled fingers.

"We happen to know a perfect fucking harbor," Krait said. "The Barracuda is going to take us past it, and we're going to swim."

"Who will be aboard her then?" Chelim asked.

"Nobody. With her sails trimmed up, she'll keep on going for days before those tub of shit navy boats catch her. Maybe she'll make land in the east someday."

She sounded hearty enough, but Tar heard an edge of grief in her voice.

Krait went to the tiller and steered the ship into a curve around the skirt of Atlantis, keeping close to the pontoons so the defenses high above wouldn't see them. Tar stood in for the crew when she called for it, adjusting the sails as she directed.

He saw tears running crooked courses among Krait's raised scars. He looked away so that she would not be ashamed.

Until now, he had not known that Krait's heart could be hurt. But this must be the worst moment of her life. She loved the Barracuda more than she loved any living person. She had lost the vessel once, then won her back. Captain and ship had been partners since Tar was an adolescent fighting in the pits.

That might also be why she had hated the idea of re-masting the ship for sail alone. It wasn't so much about oars or slaves. Rather, the notion of altering her beloved ship was an outrage. To Krait, the Barracuda had always been perfect. Such a thought hadn't occurred to Tar before.

"Ready at the rail!" she shouted, and scrubbed her wet cheeks with the back of her hand.

She lashed the tiller in place. The Barracuda would now sail straight for the horizon until the wind failed.

They sped past some commercial piers, perilously close to the ships moored along them. Then the structures fell away, revealing a crescent of water fringed with rich pleasure boats and sturdy merchant caravels, all swaddled in shreds of the rising mist.

It was the private harbor of House Mannon, the very place where Tar and Krait had won their freedom from Atlantis not long ago. Now they were returning to the same spot. As Krait had said, it was the stupidest plan possible, and therefore the only one that might work.

THE DRIPPING quartet of fugitives hauled themselves out of the water. They sheltered from view behind bales of old clothes intended to be shipped to the mainland for processing into felt. There was a great deal of activity that morning, but no one was looking for strangers rising from the sea.

"I have often dreamed of coming here with you for the first time," Chelim remarked to Abeka. "Never did I dream we'd arrive by swimming."

"Welcome to Atlantis, sweet Chelim," the princess replied.

"We need to dry off so we don't attract attention," Tar said. "After that, we can—"

"No more 'we'," Abeka said. "You already saved our lives, freed us from the Gyraf, and spoiled my uncle's wedding plans. You have done more than anyone could ask."

Tar was confused by this.

"Nobody is counting our deeds," he objected. "Your troubles have hardly even begun."

"I'm counting the shit out of our deeds," Krait amended. "There's a mastodon-sized gold buffalo in my future."

She had been staring after the sails of the Barracuda, now lost to sight in the mist.

Abeka shook her head.

"You can't spend gold if you're dead, Captain Krait Venom Libagoro of Men. The beads in my hair are carved from precious stones. With four of these braids you can buy passage back to the mainland. A safer day, I will reward you as promised."

Chelim began to object to this proposed outrage upon her mistress' coiffure, but Abeka raised her hand.

"Tar and Krait risked everything to get us here, where they are wanted for execution, and have lost all they possessed—even that brave ship. They have no friends here. Everyone in Atlantis is their enemy. I must ensure they get away to kinder shores."

"I do *not* take payment in hair," Krait said.

Tar decided to end the pointless negotiations.

"Abeka, you are mistaken. I have one friend in Atlantis. Let's disguise ourselves with these rags. Then follow me."

PART II

22

Tar had seen Rowana-Ya in every position but this one.

The proud lady knelt at Abeka's feet, her left hand on her heart, right hand behind her back, eyes cast down.

"Abeka Calyp-Ash, Princess Royal of Atlantis, I live and die at your command."

"Please rise," Abeka said. "I have never felt less royal in my life."

Rowana-Ya stood and smiled.

"Tattered shawls cannot disguise your glory."

Looking on were Krait, Tar, and Chelim. They stood inside the gates of the outer wall of Rowana-Ya's palace, where beggars came for alms. Chelim knelt to Rowana-Ya. The pirates remained on their feet.

Krait stepped forward.

"Lady Rowana-Ya of House Mannon, I live and die and so on. Sorry I threatened to kill you last time we met. In hindsight, I fucked up. It was kind of a stressful day."

"I'd forgotten," Rowana-Ya said. "That was the most

chaotic and consequential day of my life. But we're visible to the street. This is no place to talk. Come into the palace, quickly."

"No," Tar said. "It's too dangerous for you. All we ask is that you get word to the king himself—and only the king—that Princess Abeka is here. We'll keep hidden until that time. When her father replies, post a message at your harbor gate and we'll find it."

Rowana-Ya took him by the arm and pulled him into the garden behind the gate.

"Don't be fools, all of you. The king isn't here. Someone may already have recognized you. Come inside."

Abeka raised her hand.

"Lady Rowana-Ya of House Mannon, I cannot guarantee your safety if you aid us. Things may yet go ill. Death stalks my path."

"Nor can I guarantee *your* safety, Princess, but I'll do everything I can. For now, you'll be safest in my private tower."

"I don't think that's the sort of place—" Tar objected.

Rowana-Ya spared him a saucy glance.

"There are *other* rooms in the tower, dear Golden Prince."

ABEKA STOOD on Rowana-Ya's balcony and gazed out over the glittering prospect of her father's capitol. She had forgotten how magnificent Atlantis was, and how very full of life. Her childhood memories were mostly fragments— glimpses of dim, echoing corridors and gaudy rooms full of courtiers. She seldom left the grounds of the royal palace when she was a small girl, so she could scarcely recall anything else.

Tar stood beside her, eyes probing the distance like a hawk seeking prey. Abeka studied his face. He was like a knife-toothed cat, she thought. Even at rest, he was watchful.

She let her eyes drift over the hard straps of muscle on his arms and chest. He could be still and silent for hours, but the terrific strength and speed within him were always ready. She felt it now, an intangible heat or vibration, as if he contained twice the life of an ordinary man.

He noticed her attention upon him.

"This is the first time I've seen what lies in this direction," he said.

He had been on the other side of the tower before. There, the balconies faced the outer, ringed districts of the city, with the sea beyond. Here they faced inwards, toward the royal palace itself, which was called the Hub of the World.

Abeka followed his gaze toward that gleaming monument.

The palace stood in the exact geographic center of the city, its gardens encircled by many fortified walls. Its central tower, the Scepter, was nearly twice as tall as any of the others, the mightiest of the Atlantean masts rising from its organ-pipe spires. On the mast were dazzling sails patterned in blue and gold. The entire palace was clad in gold, relieved with platinum, onyx, and colorful mosaics so that it never became monotonous in its splendor.

At the foot of the palace walls was a spacious harbor, connected to the distant sea by four broad, straight inland canals that divided Atlantis into quarters. A system of locks raised the water level in these canals nearly a hundred feet from outer shore to the Hub.

There were many other palaces in a ring around the royal compound. The greatest families, of which House Mannon was one, lived closest to the center. Beyond these, lesser palaces became mansions, mansions houses, and houses *insulae*, or apartment blocks, as one got closer to the ocean. Warehouses, workshops, and slums built of rubbish made up the fringe of the city.

Tar's eyes flicked downward, attracted to some motion Abeka did not see. She searched for it in the scene below the walls of Lady Rowana-Ya's palace. The streets teemed with activity. Craftspeople, hawkers, beasts of burden, palanquins, tourists, and countless citizens swirled over the pavements. It reminded her of that day's hectic journey.

She had seen more of Atlantis on their trip than in her entire first decade of life. What she saw was at once inspiring and troubling—from the street, one witnessed how much poverty and desperation there was. From the towers, one saw only gold and glory.

But it *was* glorious. Above their vantage point on the balcony, House Mannon's mast was brilliant with white sails. All around, the masts that sprang from other great palaces were clothed in equally handsome canvas, their banners and pennants snapping in the lively air. Smoke from kitchen fires in the distant suburbs turned the geometric shadows of the city blue and hazy. White seabirds speckled the sky around them like restless stars.

"It is so beautiful," Abeka said.

"Everything is beautiful from a great height," Rowana-Ya remarked.

She had brought them a golden tray of food and wine with her own hands. Chelim was close behind her. The maid bowed and took the refreshments to a table, then poured wine.

"I've never seen such a large shrine to Ah-Ut Hur outside the royal temple grounds," Abeka said.

She pointed out the large lake that occupied nearly a quarter of the Mannon palace gardens, a splendid golden pagoda dedicated to the goddess anchored in the middle.

"It used to be a zoological garden. My late husband had a

menagerie there. I didn't like the noise the animals made at night—nor the sound of their victims."

"I pray you are not afflicted with more grief than you can bear at his loss," Abeka said.

Rowana-Ya smiled kindly—because it would have been impolite to laugh.

"You are very gracious, Your Highness. Does your maid drink wine?"

"Dear Chelim, join us," Abeka said. "My father once said 'There is no caste on the battlefield'. I didn't understand what he meant until our recent adventures. We shared every misfortune alike. To deny you anything would be to deny a sister."

Tears spilled out of Chelim's eyes. "I've too many nerves for wine, but with your permission, I shall eat some cake."

Tar had not spoken in some time.

"I think I see a route to escape on foot if things go wrong," he said, and went back inside the tower without bothering to explain.

Rowana-Ya and Abeka stood together on the balcony and were quiet for a while, each with her thoughts. Then Rowana-Ya laughed politely.

"Your Highness, pardon me. But the way you are leaning on the balustrade and gazing out to sea—you look just like a sailor on the deck of a ship."

Abeka realized she was slouching with her elbows on the rail, her weight on one leg and the other bent, the picture of insolent contrapposto. She laughed at herself.

"Look at me!" she said, and stood up properly. "My mother would be appalled. Piracy wreaked a terrible influence on my comportment."

"I've never seen anyone Uttaboraa so relaxed," Rowana-Ya said. "It's refreshing. I go to absurd lengths to be comfortable in life, yet would not sprawl in a chair or put my feet up on the table, even at knife-point."

Abeka thought of the sea journey.

"I will say—the sailor's life is entirely without comforts. They sleep on the deck regardless of the weather, they're hot or cold according to the season, and no hardship is too great to trouble them. There was a woman on the Barracuda whose teeth were knocked out, and she spent the rest of the voyage learning how to whistle through the gap."

"I see from your face that you do not regret your travails," Rowana-Ya said.

"Enduring them was miserable, but I am so glad to have done so. I was suffocating in Okré, Lady Rowana-Ya. Court life was claustrophobic. I was beginning to fall into idle habits there, gossiping and finding fault, wasting my time in petty rivalries."

"Pirate life is not that different, is it? They risk their lives, endure all that weather and suffering and bloodletting—for what? A few handfuls of stolen gold?"

"It might be the stakes that make their lives different. With my wealth and status, I risk very little, no matter what I do. Pirates spend their lives with one foot on their own deck, and the other on the deck of Atlax, the ship of the dead. Their every living moment is a risk."

"You've had a lifetime of risk in the last few weeks."

"And the greatest risk lies ahead of me. To Mazo-Mari," Abeka said, and raised her cup.

They drank and lapsed into companionable silence. After a while, without realizing it, Abeka fell back into a sailor's pose, leaning her elbows on the rail with her hip cocked, as Krait so often did.

23

Rowana-Ya could spare less than an hour before she had to descend the tower for her evening's work. She was constantly busy with the affairs of her late husband's estate as well as her own. On top of that, she now needed to employ her influence and connections to ensure Abeka's safety. Time was among her enemies.

And it must be Rowana-Ya that came up with a plan. Tar wanted to find some squalid inn and hide the princess there until she was able to make contact with someone reliable inside the royal circle. Krait wanted to kidnap someone important and make them deliver a message, perhaps with a ransom thrown in.

Atlantis would not favor those efforts, Rowana-Ya knew. If anyone was to be a reliable go-between with the inner court, it was herself. But if she spoke to the wrong person, she would also die. Kidnapping was out of the question.

It was up to her to keep the fugitives somewhere safe until she was certain whom to trust. It was possible she could trust no one, in which case they would have to wait for the return of her cousin the king from his sea voyage—and plead her case directly to him. That could take weeks or months.

But a pit-fighter, a pirate queen, and the first daughter of Atlantis would be certain to attract attention eventually. Where could she hide them?

While Rowana-Ya attended to business in the grand salon she used for a workspace, the back of her mind gnawed at the problem.

The answer came to her in the form of a Palankan merchant she despised, come to ask her for a large sum of money.

HER MAJOR DOMO Apt-Ko-Ap was a tall, slender man. He was as black as basalt, and customarily wore brilliant blue sleeves, copper-embroidered sashes, and golden ornaments in his hair and around his throat and wrists. His grace and beauty were renowned at the royal court, but Rowana-Ya had never bedded him, as he preferred the same kind of rough men she did.

"Hur Merker is here to ask you for something," Apt-Ko-Ap said. His voice was deep purple velvet.

The lady had been working through the evening's appointments without much attention, her thoughts on the princess. At the mention of that name, she became fully present.

"He disgusts me. Put him off."

"I regret to admit I've put him off three times already. He has mentioned lodging a complaint at the court. He waits in the antechamber."

"Bring him in, and remain in the room," she said.

A minute later, a big, solid figure tramped into the salon. Hur Merker appeared to have been carved from meat. He was coarse and fleshy, always purple-faced and glistening. He wore a precisely-trimmed beard that simulated a division between his neck and his head.

It wasn't his appearance that bothered Rowana-Ya. Nobody could choose their looks. It was his childish desire to annoy his betters and hurt his inferiors, which reminded her of her late husband. He considered everyone he met to be expendable in service of his whims, and didn't give a damn whether he was loved or hated.

"I live and die by your command," he lied, and bowed with such elaborate good form it was obvious he meant it mockingly.

Apt-Ko-Ap stood by the entrance to the chamber and rolled his eyes.

Rowana-Ya inclined her head, the minimum of politesse.

"May we prosper together. You wish something from me?"

"Straight to the point," he said, beaming. "I do hate small talk. Business and pleasure—what else is there worth discussing?"

His colonial accent made his words sound angular and hard. When the lady did not reply, he continued:

"Yes, I wish something indeed. You know that my underlings have struggled to keep trade routes open to the north, across the badlands to the steppes. You know there is a sea route that stretches to the east, running parallel to the badlands, and that it makes no landfall there."

"Indeed. It's on the map."

Rowana-Ya flicked her hand at a vast tapestry that covered the entire west wall. It was a flattened-out chart of the world, embroidered with every geographic detail known to man. When new lands were discovered, her seamstresses would stitch their shapes into the map. When the borders of nations changed, they would pick out the old ones and sew in the new.

Hur Merker strode up to the tapestry and touched it—probably because it was frowned upon to do so.

"You can have your slave-bitches add in some new features there," he said, pointing high up where the badlands met the sea.

"My scouts, you see, have discovered a shallow tributary of the river Eft that comes within half a mile of the shore. It was hidden in a swamp. With sufficient resources, we can dredge it deeper and dig a canal to the sea. Then we can strip the steppes of their wealth without crawling across the stone deserts from fort to fort and losing half of it to those knife-nosed bandits who infest the route."

Despite her distaste for the man, Rowana-Ya was interested in the idea. Most of Atlantis's colonies were on the west and east of the Middle Sea in that time. Palanka was in the north, at the limit of the empire.

Atlantis had long yearned to dominate the territory to the northeast of the sea beyond Palanka, but it was difficult to reach from shore. There were mountains, deserts, and ferocious peoples in the way. The commerce that came from there was limited, but fabulously rich. What Hur Merker proposed—if it was true—would allow Atlantis to thrust a dagger into the heart of that region and bleed those riches out.

"Are your scouts reliable?" she asked.

"There are none finer beneath the sun," he said. "They are led by the great Urdos Crane and Halim-Tu, who found the way to the Scarlet City that the ancestors knew not."

That was the infuriating thing about Hur Merker, she thought. He was a consummate asshole, but a genius when it came to getting results.

"And what do you ask of me? My funds are limited these days. House Mannon has been in turmoil."

The turmoil was true, but in fact she'd never been richer.

She intended to refuse his request out of spite, no matter how attractive it might be. She wanted to upset him more than she wanted the potential of a good return on investment.

He approached the couch on which she reclined, bent forward until his face was a little too close to hers, and kneaded his hands together.

"Funds? I hardly consider what I ask to be funds. It's purse-money to you who are so wealthy."

"I'll be the judge of that," she said, stiffly.

His breath smelled of peppercorns. Typically only the poor chewed these, to mute hunger pangs.

"You know that I am but a humble merchant. I rent a hovel from you, yet to me it is a palace. Otherwise I would finance the mission myself and reap the entire reward. Alas, I can barely feed my scanty harem, I am so poor."

She knew he was enormously rich for a commoner without titles, owning as he did a quarter of a million acres in Palanka, complete with a castle. He rented a mansion from her in Atlantis because it was convenient to his docks, not because he couldn't afford his own place. He simply wasn't in town often enough to merit buying property.

Because she said nothing, he made his pitch.

"I humbly beg you for a mere two million, six hundred thousand, four hundred gold serpents," he said. "Not a copper crab more."

"That's enough to build a city. Do you intend to found an empire in the steppes?"

"It's scarcely enough to get my ships there," he laughed. "If you were younger and hungrier, you'd know the price of everything has gone up."

She felt the insult to her age—and possibly her weight— just as he intended.

She was about to send him away, when she realized the

voyage he planned would leave his mansion in Atlantis without a master, but fully staffed—a complete household, ready to move into, teeming with female slaves. A perfect disguise.

She took a deep breath.

"Hur Merker, if you are not otherwise occupied, perhaps we can dine together," she said. "I have some acquaintances in need of suitable lodgings, and you are in need of money; I think a deal could be struck."

Apt-Ko-Ap's handsome face was frozen in an expression of absolute shock. Merker beamed with delight.

24

———

As soon as the meeting ended, Apt-Ko-Ap rushed up the tower to inform the fugitives of the sudden dinner plan. Krait was to remain on guard with the princess. Tar would dine with a guest. Rowana-Ya had whispered some detailed instructions to the major domo, which he conveyed to Tar:

"She asks you not to be provoked by this man," he said. "He will try to sting you. No matter what, you must not raise a word—or a hand—against him. He is the answer to your problem, she says. She did not mention how."

There was no question of Abeka attending the meal. Merker might recognize her, as her portrait was carved in many places about the city.

Tar immediately accompanied Apt-Ko-Ap down to the feasting hall. Rowana-Ya made the introduction, placing her hands on theirs to formally connect them through her person.

"Hur Merker, this is Tar Okré of Men. May we prosper together."

Hur Merker bowed. Tar did the same, equally insincerely.

"It is always a pleasure to meet a fellow colonial," Merker said. "You know how it is with business. Atlanteans can be so idealistic. We must be hard-headed."

Tar did not know how it was with business, but nodded all the same. He reclined at the dining table alongside Rowana-Ya, opposite Hur Merker, as she indicated he should.

"Hur Merker and I were discussing the unrest in Palanka," she said. "The natives rose up over wages because they receive no profits from their resources. He has strong opinions on the matter, with which I am certain you will agree."

The last part was aimed straight at Tar. This was not the time for taking an anti-exploitation stance.

He nodded.

Merker laughed, his small eyes twinkling.

"A man of few words. Suits me well."

The meal itself was easy enough to get through. Tar had never been served at table before. Impeccably mannered slave-women came and went in a continuous file, like ants. Every task but the eating itself was performed by them—the arrival and departure of courses, cutting and serving, application of sauces and condiments, refreshing of goblets, and the whisking-away and replacement of soiled trenchers.

Tar had no idea what he was supposed to do, so he simply waited until they stopped fussing with his portions, then ate until they took them away. Simple enough. The food was good, but far too complex for his simple palate to appreciate.

Only once did she correct his behavior. He thanked a slave for topping up his wine and she pinched his ankle with her naked toes beneath the table.

"Slaves are invisible," she whispered. "They should receive no thanks or acknowledgment."

Merker observed Tar's error, and insolently called the same slave over to refill his own cup. He moved his goblet in mid-pour, and expected the girl not to spill any. When a single droplet fell to the linen, he slapped her sharply on the thigh.

"In Palanka the slaves know their work," he said, and toasted the party: "I raise my glass to we who turn labor into gold."

Tar drank sparingly. He'd been drunk often enough aboard the Barracuda, but that was when long days passed with no events to mark them. Now that every minute could bring opportunity or disaster, he wanted to be in full command of his faculties at all times. And he could not risk letting loose his temper.

At first, the Palankan and Rowana-Ya talked business. Tar nodded along as if he understood. As the wine took hold, Hur Merker began to drift into boastful anecdotes.

He told stories of his conquests—mines dug and emptied, plantations carved from forests, fleets of ships so stuffed with slaves that they couldn't lie down the entire voyage to Atlantis. He described his harem, and how he fucked each woman in a different position. He talked of the upcoming voyage and what fortunes slept in the arms of the unsuspecting natives of the steppes, whom he would soon plunder.

How this man could possibly be helpful to Abeka's cause, Tar could not imagine. If he was the answer to their current difficulties, it was a small price to tolerate him for a few hours. Still, the man was an unbearable swamp-hog.

"If this expedition is successful," Merker concluded, "I estimate it will return your investment handsomely."

Rowana-Ya nodded and grinned in a conspiratorial way.

"I do not doubt you for a moment," she purred. "I have decided to fund your expedition, on condition that Tar's traveling-party may dwell in your mansion for a week or two. They are visiting Atlantis, and find no suitable lodgings close to their harbor."

"As long as this Okré fellow doesn't crap on the floor, of course. I'm told they do that in your parts."

He sneered at Tar.

Tar reached for the short knife tucked into his sash. Rowana-Ya grasped his wrist with her soft hand and used all her strength to keep him from drawing the blade. The struggle lasted several seconds, hidden beneath the tabletop. He could easily have overpowered her, but recalled her warning: Do not let the man goad him. He relaxed his muscles and placed his hand on the table.

If Hur Merker saw what happened, he didn't remark on it. He owed his life to their hostess, not Tar's self-control.

25

───────────

All evenings must end. When the moonrise bell rang, Tar rose from his couch sober. The Palankan was so drunk a manservant had to help him stand up. Despite his condition, he lingered to chat, leaving only when he was certain he'd overstayed his welcome.

Tar had given Hur Merker no reason to like or dislike him. He was an incidental character; the main topic in the merchant's mind was Rowana-Ya's money, overshadowing all else. The man would probably forget him before he reached home—scarred and brooding ruffians like Tar were as common as rats in Atlantis, although they seldom had such leonine eyes.

Rowana-Ya accompanied Tar in the lift back to her suite. They spoke in low tones as the gilded, clanking cage rose up the mast that formed the trunk of the tower. She set it to ascend at its lowest speed—the lift was the only truly private place in the entire palace, now that she had guests in her private apartments.

"Thank you for enduring that boor. It was necessary he meet you."

"I shouldn't have let him anger me."

"There's anger in the air, lately. All of Atlantis is in a mood. One can almost taste it on hot days. I am in a state myself. I'm always tense, like I'm expecting bad news."

"Other than harboring the princess, what's the matter?"

"There's some sort of intrigue in the royal palace which I can't get anyone to reveal. None of my spies know anything. The inner circle has sealed itself in, even against close cousins of the king such as I."

"It has to be about the princess," Tar said. "Someone opened a clear path through the treasure barge for the assassins who came to kill her. She says few people could arrange such a thing."

"*Very* few, it's true. I couldn't even manage it. It has to be someone in the immediate royal family, or one of their closest attendants. If Duke Illusan was scheming to marry her, perhaps the youngest brother wants her dead. He loses a great deal of power after such a union."

"Maybe Illusan himself wanted her dead," Tar said.

"But why?"

"I don't know. You Uttaboraa are as twisted as rope. Abeka told me this is how you spend your time. Always scheming against each other. Nothing better to do."

"It's our only source of excitement, other than sexual deviancy. But this time it's different. The king has been at sea leading the navy for nearly three months. Both of his brothers are here in Atlantis. It's a recipe for poison. When dynasties in-fight, there is a fine line between a conflict and a coup. This wedding was supposed to be the start of something, not the end. What that is, I cannot guess."

She pulled an ivory lever and the lift stopped short of her suite. She took him by the shoulders, her hands barely spanning his deltoid muscles, and looked into his eyes.

"Golden Prince, I must say this. Please do not hate me for it."

"I make no promises."

"It's too dangerous for Princess Abeka outside the royal palace. I want you to hand her over to her mother."

"That's not what she wants."

"My loyalty lies with her parents, not her."

Tar punched the cage around them, making it rock on its suspension chains.

"I don't give a damn where your loyalties lie. It's up to the princess, not you or me."

She caught his chin in her hand.

"That's a bold statement, coming from one of the most wanted criminals in Atlantis. Are you in a position to argue with me?"

His face went cold and his tawny eyes flashed with a killing light. He had not survived this long by showing mercy to those who threatened him—regardless of whom they were.

"I'm in a position to break your neck."

She scoffed.

"You wouldn't dare kill me."

The corner of his mouth twitched, but he suppressed the smile. It was worse than any threat.

She let go of his jaw and wrapped her arms around herself as if the sultry night had grown cold.

"Even me," she said.

He relented—slightly.

"The princess paid us to keep her out of her uncle's hands," he said. "So that's what we're doing. It's not idealism, it's gold."

Rowana-Ya shook her head.

"I'm not naive, child. You don't care about the money. You care about freedom. You're doing this because you are compelled to set her free from the trap she's in. You could never have done otherwise."

The murder drained out of his eyes.

"Don't call me child."

"Then stop sulking like one. You're still in your teens, aren't you? Both hands of one, hand of another?"

"*And* both thumbs, finger of another."

"Eighteen. My Gods, you're only a year older than my son when he died."

"Make this cage go again. There's nothing more to talk about. The princess stays with us. We will leave immediately. I can't trust you."

Her eyes brimmed with tears. Tar did not know why. She placed her palm on his chest, which he knew was her gesture of tenderness.

"My Prince," she said, and smiled with genuine warmth, "you are extraordinary—an exceptionally dangerous, clever, ambitious, and fearless boy. The kind that becomes a great leader, if he lives past thirty. Yet a boy nonetheless. This desire to rescue the princess is an idealistic fantasy. You'd know this, if you were in your full manhood."

"Are you talking about my cock?"

She laughed, and the tears of sorrow turned to mirth and spilled down her cheeks.

She certainly was in a state, he thought.

"Be patient, my Prince," she said. "Atlantis robbed you of your childhood."

She stepped back and stood tall and straight, shoulders squared. The regal blood in her showed through. She tilted up her chin:

"I will say it once more, and then never again. If you kill me, so be it: please allow me to bring the princess home to her mother. Where else will she be safe?"

Tar was about to object, but she raised her hand: *Let me finish*.

"Golden Prince, why do you not set *yourself* free, by turning the princess over to her parent? She will only be returning to her rightful place. Your crimes will be forgiven. You'll be rewarded with the gold you pretend to desire. Then you can live whatever life you choose, free of all the horror you have endured. Everyone lives in that scenario. Nobody lives in yours."

"It's not up to me," he said.

She restarted the lift, and within moments they had ascended into her private quarters.

26

"Tell them what you told me," Tar said, when the fugitives had gathered in Rowana-Ya's private salon.

Outside, the darkness below was spangled with countless lamps and torches. Atlantis slept in shifts. When the night cooled, the citizens would ascend to their rooftops to enjoy the air. They cooked, mended, and danced by firelight. The trail of stars that arched through the purple-black heavens seemed to fall straight into the sea.

Tar looked out at it, his back to the room, as their hostess repeated what she had begged him to do.

"Krait, you would be rich. Your partner doesn't care for gold, but *you* do. And Princess, no place in my estates is secure enough to guarantee your safety. The royal palace is right there, barely a springbow-shot away. I beg you allow me to escort you home to your closest family. My entire garrison will guard your way."

"With the greatest respect, Lady Mannon, my closest family includes the uncle who would wed me to usurp my father's power—and someone unknown who would see me killed."

"But the marriage plot is foiled! And what assassin could penetrate to the very heart of the mightiest citadel in Atlantis?"

"Any of my people," Krait said. "Your security ain't shit."

"But your people would never raise a hand against She Who Won the War With a Single Stroke."

"Don't bullshit us, Lady. I understand what you're worried about. You're harboring fugitives and the heir to the Atlantean throne under your roof. It doesn't matter what your politics are. You don't like the exposure."

"At court we're most loyal to those whom we fear. I fear her uncle right down to my marrows."

Tar turned around.

"We'll be gone within the hour."

Rowana-Ya bit at her knuckle for a few moments, then committed.

"In that case, I will tell you why I introduced you to that Palankan pig. He departs on a long sea voyage tomorrow, so his mansion will be available, and all his slaves. It is in the Old Captain's Quarter, a part of the city convenient to shipping—including my own harbor. The Summer Canal cleaves through it, so there's a straight path to the royal palace."

"Too many eyes on us," Tar said. "We need to disappear."

"And so you shall," Rowana-Ya said. "You will play roles."

"We've been doing that already," Abeka said. "Pretending I don't have a title."

"You have to take it to its limits, Princess. For example, Tar will pose as a master, because Atlantis is searching for a slave. Krait, you pose as a lady—because you are not one."

"Did you just fucking insult me?"

Krait was irritated—she had hoped to spend the night in the luxury of the palace tower.

"*Are* you a lady?" Rowana-Ya asked.

"Fair point. What about Her Highness?"

The lady turned to Abeka and knelt before her.

"My princess, I regret even to speak these words, but I see no other disguise that will keep you as safe. Because you are the farthest thing from a slave—you must pretend to be one."

Chelim nearly threw herself off the balcony at this suggestion, but Abeka merely nodded.

"You are wise, my lady," she said. "I shall do as you suggest. Chelim, calm yourself. It is no insult. We are in mortal danger here, and must go unobserved."

Chelim stamped her feet, but the richly carpeted floor made no sound.

"I will not allow it! You are the heir to all Atlantis! To live like a slave, to share their work—it is obscene. Better that we should die."

"What's your problem with slaves?" Tar asked, a hint of razor in his voice.

"I apologize," Chelim said, and hung her head.

"How about Chelim plays my servant for a while?" Krait said. "She doesn't need to be anything other than what she is, but slaves don't have servants."

"A fine suggestion," Rowana-Ya replied. "Hur Merker's mansion has private quarters for guests. Krait, you and Chelim can stay there as Tar's guests, he'll pretend to be Hur Merker's brother or something like that, and Princess Abeka can conceal herself among his slaves—all beautiful women, according to him."

"That's well enough," Tar said, "but we can't sit there in his house and play dice forever. What's the plan of action?"

"I will waste no time in learning whom we can trust with the news that you are here in Atlantis, and whom it was that tried to have you assassinated. Until then, you play dice. Two or three days. A week. Be patient."

"I say we do it," Abeka said.

"Krait?" Tar asked.

"Fuck it. I'll play the lady for a while."

Rowana-Ya drew breath for the first time in what seemed like five minutes.

"Thank you. If the Gods smile upon us, we may succeed. Now—I would have private speech with the Golden Prince next door, if you will excuse us. There are separate matters I would discuss with him."

KRAIT WENT DOWN to the gardens to brood over the loss of the Barracuda.

Rowana's private suite in the tower was divided into four parts arranged around the mast, with three of them devoted to a spacious bedchamber, drawing room, and salon for entertaining guests. The fourth contained the bathing-room and winter bedroom in which the fugitives were camped.

She nearly always slept in the winter bedroom, as the larger one with its enormous bed was devoted to her sexual adventures. It was to this cushioned expanse Tar carried her.

There was nothing to discuss. They made each other's bodies ready standing up. The foreplay didn't end until Rowana-Ya's knees gave out. After that, it was war.

The two bedrooms shared a wall, and Rowana-Ya had ensured the wall was insulated against sound. But there was no glazing in the large bedchamber. Consequently, when the balcony doors of the winter bedroom were open, everything was audible between them.

Tar didn't know this, and Rowana-Ya didn't care. So Abeka and Chelim were treated to a symphony of passion. Randomly-timed thumps and crashes, long intervals of rhythmic pounding, and the throaty cries of their hostess tormented the eavesdropper's ears. They were at once morti-fied, fascinated, and amused.

"What did she say?" Abeka whispered. "Wait, she's saying it again."

"I can't take any more?"

They giggled into their hands.

Then Tar spoke, which he hadn't done so far:

"You'll take what I give you."

Rowana-Ya cried out in agony, or something like it. For a long while, their hostess only shouted 'fuck' over and over again.

"Should we call the guards?" Chelim whispered. She was afraid.

"I don't know. Back in Okré, nobody has sex like this," Abeka said. "But this is what it sounded like when Captain Krait went below deck with her sailors, and they survived well enough."

They knew killing didn't take this long. As Rowana-Ya kept on shouting and moaning, she must not be dying.

The women remained where they were, listening. Both of them felt the erotic charge in the air. It was a delicious unease that concentrated below their bellies and lifted the fine hairs on their skin.

Although virginal, they knew what sex was—they weren't ignorant of life. But this was not sex as they had read in stories and heard in songs, where it was the pure culmina-tion of love. This was the sex of beasts. Beasts with human voices.

"Say you missed me," they heard Rowana-Ya beg. "Say you care for me at all."

"You're nothing to me—like all you worthless Uttaboraa whores," Tar snarled, and renewed his pounding attack.

Abeka's face went ashen at his words.

"It's just talk," Chelim said. "He didn't mean you."

"He meant me most of all," Abeka said, and closed the shutters of the winter bedroom—not to escape the sound of the lovemaking next door, but to muffle her own sobs.

27

In the morning, there was no trace of Abeka's grief. With great misgivings, Tar agreed they should go to Hur Merker's mansion by separate ways. Krait and Chelim would arrive first, so that the pirate could suss out any potential dangers in advance. If anything seemed off, she would turn Tar and Abeka away at the door.

The two parties left by different gates of Rowana-Ya's palace, and she did not see them off. To do so might arouse curiosity.

Krait could never be mistaken for a lady of good birth, but she made up for it with swagger. When she walked through the crowded, dirty, noisy streets, people got out of her way. Merchants she passed would hawk their wares to her, ignoring everyone else. Crusty-nosed street urchins would stare after her. It wasn't the scarification or her intricately embroidered sash that drew attention. It was her supreme confidence.

"You're too obvious," Chelim whispered from behind her.

"Too obviously top shit?"

"Everyone is gawking at you. You just absolutely radiate pirate."

"What the fuck am I supposed to do? Radiate camel-dealer?"

"I don't know! Act normal!"

Krait stopped and turned on Chelim, who walked into her. The maid apologized and bowed very low. Krait pulled her behind a towering pile of seal skins, the most private place in the street.

"Normal is for pussies. What I don't understand is if I'm a rich captain and you're my servant, how do I treat you? What do I do? I've never had a servant."

"That depends on how you feel about me."

"I'd love to feel about you."

"Don't be shameless. I mean whether I'm close to you or only a member of your staff."

"I haven't decided yet. Tell you what. I promise I won't cause a scene from here to the address. No fighting, no killing."

"And no shouting."

"Deal. Relax, girl. Nobody is going to think I'm on the wanted list."

"How can you be so certain?"

"Because I'm too obviously top shit."

Chelim begged her at least to hire a palanquin to take them the rest of the way. Krait liked the idea—she'd never ridden in one before. They went in style, carried in the box by six well-ordered bearers. The elevated perspective gave them a fine view of the streets.

Krait was delighted to discover the Captain's Quarter, which was well-furnished with drinking-houses, brothels, and chandlers where all the finest ship's gear could be found.

"We're going to explore this fucking place while we're

here," she said, and playfully punched Chelim on the shoulder —with enough force to knock the wind out of a warthog. Chelim bounced off the wall of the palanquin and cringed.

"Trogo's balls, are you *afraid* of me?" Krait snorted.

"Of course I'm afraid of you. You kill people to amuse yourself."

"Lots of people do that. What else?"

"You shout a lot and make horrible threats. You care nothing for human life. And you have a terrible sense of humor. On the Barracuda I saw you set fire to a sailor's buttock hair for a joke."

"Oh Gods, the *smell*. It was hilarious, for fuck's sake."

"And you use such terrible language."

Krait was in a magnanimous mood—and horny.

"By the weeping fistula of the Scorpion Queen," she declared, "if my behavior offends you, I will mend my ways. Temporarily."

Chelim removed herself from the corner.

"Thank you."

"Tell me something. I've had many fucking—sorry, many slaves, but never a servant. What's the fu— Shit. The difference? Am I not allowed to beat you?"

Chelim rubbed her shoulder.

"The difference is caste," Chelim said, and proudly elaborated:

"I am Kabira-Kabra, second degree of freemen. I can inherit land, seek new employment at my discretion, and am guaranteed paid holidays during the festivals of Mazo-Mari, Ah-Ut-Hur, Ancestor's Eve, and the Vernal Equinox. Also my death qualifies as murder according to law."

"That's it?"

Chelim had hoped to impress Krait with her status, as she'd begun life as Kabra, lowest caste of freemen. But she should have known better. Krait was only impressed by fast ships, gold, and spectacular acts of violence.

"My caste is all I truly possess," she said, deflated.

Krait wanted to keep things cheerful.

"Don't get me wrong, I'm fu— happy for you. It's just that my fu— people don't have castes, so I'm not versed in the subject. How high up the fu... ladder is Kabira-Kabra?"

"Only seventh from the very top!" Chelim was proud again.

"How many below you?"

"Five."

"So you're damn near halfway there."

Krait meant this in an encouraging way. She was trying very hard to be agreeable, as she fully intended to seduce the maid at the earliest possible opportunity. Being agreeable was not easy. She would need to beat someone up soon. She needed to say 'fuck'.

They reached Hur Merker's street and stepped down from the palanquin. For better or worse, it was time to play house.

28

———————

The young scarred mercenary and his proud slave-woman were in no hurry to get anywhere. They wore salt-stained, hooded sea cloaks which showed they'd only just arrived in Atlantis. By her bearing, the woman must have been captured from some high-born mainland household. The man must have captured the woman himself—he wasn't rich enough to have bought such a fine specimen.

If there was anything unusual about them, it was that she had the features of a pure Atlantean. She wasn't of colonial blood. Then again, any house could fall, and anyone could become a slave.

The mercenary sauntered through the crowded street with one hand resting on the jeweled pommel of a saber, the other holding a leather rein that ended in a silver torc around the slave's neck. She had probably attempted to escape once too often.

"We'll stop here," he said, coming to an arcaded building with tables and benches lining the covered porch.

He sat facing the street, slouched heavily against the brass wall with his legs splayed out wide. She sat beside him where he slapped the bench, prim as a vase of flowers.

The tavern was busy and chaotic inside, but men like him were served quickly regardless of the trade. A barman in traditional floor-length apron brought a jug of seaweed beer for him and a cup of sweet vinegar-water for her.

"Now we sit here and pretend we have nowhere to be," Tar said in a low voice.

"There's a doorway on my right and a window on your left. If anything happens, go in the window and come out the door and run toward the palace like T'hoth himself was after you."

"Should we be sitting out in the open like this?"

"We've been walking for half an hour. It's time to learn if anyone walks with us."

He studied the passing scene from beneath the fringe of his hood, his features hidden behind the jug perpetually at his lips.

Tar had been memorizing faces the entire walk, noting who turned with them at intersections and who looked their way, anyone and anything suspicious. So far, nobody had caught his notice more than twice. three times and he'd take them down a dark alley, just to be on the cautious side. Atlantis had countless such alleys, and that's where most bodies were found.

"I don't know how you can drink that vile stuff," Abeka said.

"Better than fish blood," he muttered.

Nobody was near enough to hear them speak, but they kept their voices down.

"I don't believe we are followed," he said, after some minutes had passed. "I'm going insane sitting here. Next we'll find a frog-catcher to guide us to Hur Merker's street.

We go to a different house. Once the child is gone, we can go to his."

'FROG-CATCHER' was a generic term for an orphan, of which there were countless in Atlantis. They could be found with their hand-made wire tridents, wading in the public canals. Salt-water frogs were worth half a copper crab per pair, as they were a nuisance, like the rats they were originally imported to hunt.

Frog-catchers also delivered messages and acted as guides, intimate with their local area in every detail. Their knowledge of the streets was famous, and the older children could often guide someone all the way across Atlantis, not just around their native quarter.

The one who now walked in front of Tar and Abeka was a girl of six years, naked except for one outsized sleeve. In Atlantis it didn't matter what you wore, but that you had something to wear. She carried her frog spear upright like a soldier.

"You look like a dargus," Tar said to the girl.

He was referring to the pit-fighters who wore an armored sleeve of leather on their right arm and carried forked javelins.

"I'm not," the girl said. But she began to swagger as she walked, not unlike Tar.

"Keep up, woman," he said, when Abeka fell back to the end of her leash.

He hated his role.

"It's here," the frog-catcher said, and pointed at a row of old but well-crafted mansions set back behind small, high-walled gardens.

Tar gave her two copper crabs, which was twice what the

service was worth, and the girl scampered away before he could decide to take the excess back.

Tar looked up and down the street.

"Now, which one is it? I hope I didn't hurt you with this accursed leash."

"I'm not made of glass," Abeka said. "Master," she added. It sounded ridiculous coming from her mouth. She might just as well have called him 'pet'.

"We're never going to get away with this," Tar growled. "You're obviously a queen. Can't you be more slave-like?"

"How?"

"Be less magnificent. I think it's this one with the two pepper trees," he added, and approached a tall copper-inlaid gate.

Before they reached it, the gate swung open and Krait stepped out, her arms draped around the necks of two beautiful slave-women clad only in skirts.

"Not a bad place you have here, Chief," she said, and ate a date out of one slave's hand.

The other chased it down with an offering of wine.

"Welcome, Cousin Merker," said a third slave.

She was tall and regal herself, her brows thick, her skin symmetrically patterned light and dark. An Arkhan from the western deserts, the Dappled Folk as they were known.

"I am Orav," she said, "over-slave to these. Come inside, Master. Name your wishes and they will be met. We will make up a bath for you and a bed for your slave. The household awaits."

Krait pressed her ivory jabbo-box into Tar's hand.

"Take this. I think you're going to need it," she said, and winked.

29

Tar sat uncomfortably on a couch in Hur Merker's spacious home, Abeka standing obediently behind him. The decor was original to the property, rich and well-worn, with the sinuous copper-and-gold vine patterns and dark upholstered walls fashionable a century before.

In front of him was Hur Merker's entire staff. It was all women, as the man had boasted: two cooks, three helpmaids, a chambermaid, a porter, and nine seraglios—his harem. Orav was part of this group, in addition to acting as head of household in his absence.

All of them except the porter were beautiful, and the porter had been beautiful until someone knocked out her left eye. Each woman was exotic in a different way from the next, so the effect was of a collection of prize specimens. Precisely what Hur Merker had in mind.

"We welcome you, Master," said all of them in unison, and bowed. "We live and die at your command."

This was literally true for slaves.

"Thanks," Tar said. "I'm Tar of Okré, cousin of Hur Merker."

He hated this performance. He glanced up at Abeka for assistance and she leaned down to whisper in his ear:

"Tell them to go about their business and do as they always do. It's best if you make a demand as well, such as feed you or wash you."

"I'm not a helpless infant," Tar whispered back, then spoke aloud:

"Uh—Go do what you do. If I need anything I'll let you know."

A couple of the women giggled at this half-hearted mastery, but all trotted away to their places except Orav, whose place was within earshot of whomever she served.

"May I speak freely, Master?" she asked.

Her melodic nomad's accent was highly attractive to Tar's ear. He glanced up at Abeka again, but she was staring fixedly ahead, trying to look like a slave.

"I suppose so," he said.

"I see that you are not accustomed to having a household of your own, Master."

"That's right. Only her," he said.

"We are all here to serve you, no matter how trivial the whim. Do not feel constrained, please, Master."

"In that case, can you not call me 'master'?"

Orav was surprised by this. "What then, would you be called?"

"My name will do."

"I cannot. It is too familiar. Although I feel I have seen you somewhere before."

"Then call me by my ship's rank—Chief," he said.

It would have to suffice.

"Shall I show your slave her quarters, Chief?" Orav said.

She spoke 'chief' as if it was a lover's joke between them.

"Please do," Tar said, and then remembered he wasn't supposed to say 'please'. He went on:

"Her name is Bek and she is of great value, so don't trouble her in any way."

Abeka stood silently while Orav looked her over like a parrot she might buy.

"Very pure blood," Orav said, appraisingly. "She is of good Atlantean stock."

"Not anymore," Abeka replied.

"Shut your mouth, Slave!" Orav barked. "Silence!"

Abeka jumped. Tar saw she was furious, about to talk back.

"Go to your quarters, Slave," he said, cutting off her objections. "Show her there," he added, to Orav.

Orav bowed deeply. Abeka took the opportunity to glare at Tar in shock and outrage for a moment. Then she sank her emotions out of sight and followed Orav into the inner rooms of the mansion.

TAR HAD NOTHING TO DO, and a dozen women to do it with him. After several attempts by Orav, he was convinced to bathe. There was a splendid tub in the master bedchamber. He watched the harem fill it with hot water, each steaming kettle requiring much bending and posturing. Did it take nine women to draw a bath?

Once they had completed the task, they tried to disrobe him. Although his cock was hard as stone, he refused their questing fingers. One thing Rowana-Ya had failed to explain to him was the rule about fucking another man's slaves.

And these were not free people. To fuck them would be to abuse his power as a freeman. Even though they appeared to want him, wasn't that their purpose? They might hate him with all their souls, yet they must pretend to be wild with desire. He had to admit they were highly skilled at pretending. Nevertheless, he would not give in to lust if it meant giving up his principles.

He shooed his gorgeous tormentors out of the room, and took off his sash and loincloth. He opened the ivory jabbo box Krait had given him. It was full. He settled himself into the bath, hoping the hot water would ease his aching balls.

There came a knock at the door. He groaned, then muttered:

"Enter."

Was there any word that didn't make him think of sex?

Abeka stepped into the room.

"I HAVE COME to scrub your back, Master," she said, closing the doors behind her.

"No you haven't," Tar said. "How are your quarters? Do those strumpets treat you kindly?"

"May I come closer, Master?"

"Stop with the slave talk. It's not funny. Sit on that bench."

The princess sat, upright and regal. She was quiet for a while, staring at Tar with the fearless gaze of one whose birthright was the entire world.

For his part, Tar stared through the balcony doors at the tops of the pepper trees, willing his prick to sleep.

"The slave quarters are simple but clean. The kitchen is immaculate and well-equipped. As for the household, I have never met a group of women so bored in my entire life—and boredom is a fine art at court in Okré. So these may be the most bored women in all the world."

"They do seem...restless," Tar agreed.

"They are bored in a particular way," she added.

"How so?"

"All they talked about in the slave quarters is your physique—and particularly your penis. They say it appears prodigiously large, and asked me many questions concerning your prowess as a lover."

Tar considered drowning himself in the bath.

"I'm told house slaves love spicy talk," he said. "They have little else to season their bland days."

"When we swam that one afternoon in the ocean off the Barracuda, I do remember thinking it was very big."

He could barely find his voice.

"What game are you playing? This is not how princesses behave, is it? We can't have this conversation."

"I know you won't ravish me, Tar."

"But it seems like you want me to."

"What if I do?" she said, her voice a whisper.

She ought to act like frigid royalty, not a woman Tar could conceivably bed. Tar could only imagine the elaborate death Atlantis would prepare for him if he deflowered its one and only royal princess.

"By the Nameless Gods," he said, "we cannot flirt with each other. Let us discuss anything else."

"Am I flirting?"

"How would I know? I know only how to kill and sail."

She bit her thumbnail, unexpectedly shy.

"But you seemed to be flirting with me, too."

"I deeply regret it."

"Do you?"

"I repeat: let's discuss anything else. Explain what kind of princess you are."

Now she raised a skeptical eyebrow.

"My titles and all that?"

"There are many princesses. What makes you the highest one?"

She lay down on the bench with one arm folded under her head—a sailor's pose.

"There's a dull topic," she said.

"Exactly."

She sighed, then recited:

"Because I am daughter to the king, I am eligible to rule from the Throne of Mazo-Mari, which is also called the Seat of Kings, where my father now sits."

She spelled this out in the air with her free hand.

"He would perch me on the throne when I was a toddler, and place the circlet of Ah-Ut Hur on my head. Apparently, I'd kick my feet and shout nonsense orders at the guards."

She smiled at the past. There had been happiness in her family once.

Tar, to his credit, was trying to follow her explanation.

"Does this mean you could be queen *without* a king?"

"Yes. There are different ranks," she said, "even among queens. I am princess royal now. If I take the Throne of Mazo-Mari on my own, I am queen regnant."

"Then you can do whatever you want."

"No, because Atlantis doesn't trust its queens, only its kings. There is a Noble Senate that would vet all my decisions. For real authority, I would have to marry a prince—then he would become king and I would become queen consort instead of regnant, and then I'd only have to convince him to do my bidding."

"Instead of the whole Noble Senate?"

"Yes. But my mother is queen consort, and she can't convince my father to do anything he doesn't already wish. So it's a precarious existence."

Tar was beginning to grasp the concept.

"Is that why Okré is technically yours, but your uncle Illusan rules the place?"

"Exactly."

"So if he marries you, he becomes king of all Atlantis."

"Once my father has died, yes."

"Maybe the Senate is a good idea," Tar thought aloud "Kings and queens should be limited in their power, so when someone like your uncle comes along, he can't ruin everything."

His cock was relaxing.

"I agree with you," she said. "Since our recent adventures, I've come to understand an old Atlantean saying—'no king without a slave'. I thought it was a clever epigram, but I know now it is literal truth. We cannot have kings if we wish to end slavery."

"The king or queen who ends it will be popular with the common folk," Tar said. "They'd keep the title."

"And be assassinated within a day. The only way slavery will end in Atlantis is with a revolution."

"Even so, for the first time, I wish I was a prince," Tar said. "So we could know each other better."

"There are two other kinds of queen," Abeka said, hurrying past his unexpected earnestness. "Queen matriarch, which my mother will become if I rule. Right now she is queen regent, which means she rules while my father is at sea commanding the navy."

"You said she was queen consort."

"She's queen consort when Father is home, queen regent when he's away, and queen matriarch when I become queen regnant."

Tar's cock was asleep at last.

"It's best if we talk of things like that," he said. "Subjects that aren't too personal."

Her voice was thick with regret.

"I suppose you're right, Tar," she said.

"But we could be here for hands of days. If not with… personal matters, how do we pass the time? I do not handle idleness well."

"Here's something useful," she said, brightening. "Let me teach you to count with numbers."

30

Chelim was restless that night. She couldn't sit down. Krait poured cups of herbed wine and gave one to her.

"Sit," she said. "You need to relax."

"I cannot. What are they talking about in there?"

For hours, there had been a constant murmur between Abeka and Tar. They had shut themselves into the master's quarters, then the conversation had begun.

"You're worried she's into him, and she'll forget about you," Krait said.

Chelim turned on her.

"That is an infamous suggestion!"

"I knew it. You're all insecure and turned on at the same time. I can tell."

The maid sat among the pile of floor cushions Atlanteans favored over chairs, her arms wrapped around her knees, her chin resting on top of them.

"Don't be vulgar, please."

"We don't have to talk, Girl," Krait said. "But you're so

tense it hurts to look at. Let's at least get your shoulders down off of your ears."

She knee-walked over the cushions and came up behind the restless servant. Her slender fingers were strong as steel from years of sailing and fighting. She dug them deep into Chelim's tight shoulder muscles, savoring the yield of her tender skin.

"Don't touch me," Chelim gasped. "Do not. Oh Gods, that feels so good."

Krait kept working in silence until the maid's shoulders were loose and her arms had fallen away from her knees. Chelim rolled her head from side to side.

"I had no idea how tense I was. You're right."

"Now breathe a minute," Krait said. "Lie back and breathe in through your nose and out through your mouth. We'll do nothing but breathe. Go ahead."

Krait lay back on the cushions and stretched like a panther, then folded her hands behind her head and did as she said. Long, dream-like breaths. After a few moments, Chelim seemed to decide there was no harm in breathing. She lay down beside Krait, close enough that their hips touched.

"That's right," Krait said. "Breathe."

She hoped the maid wouldn't sense her own arousal—she was struggling not to climb on top of the woman and start grinding. But seduction wasn't hunting, it was poaching. The trick was to set the trap and let the prey walk into it.

"You're feeling better, I can tell. Let's drink to the princess."

Krait propped herself up on her elbow and playfully touched her cup to Chelim's lips. Pale wine ran down the maid's cheeks.

"Oh, now I'm wet," she said, but giggled despite herself.

Krait drank from the cup.

"Can I ask you something?"

"It depends," Chelim said.

She was as mellow now as Krait had ever seen her, but still fenced around with the habit of propriety.

"You know how it is with me," Krait said, her voice low and honeyed. "I'm not exactly shy about it. But... have you ever lain with anyone?"

Chelim was mortified. She sat up again.

"Never!"

"Is it not allowed? I mean are you like the Sisters of the Moon, who have to stay virginal?"

Krait had once convinced a Sister of the Moon to break her vow of chastity, which is why she was aware of such things.

"Everything is permitted me," Chelim said. "But I cannot serve Her Majesty as she deserves if my attention is turned to my own gratification."

"Then again," Krait purred, "you know they're probably getting busy next door. If she's exploring the physical side of things, shouldn't you? Otherwise, you can't be properly supportive. You'll fall behind."

"I hadn't thought of that. She'll treat me like a child."

Krait idly ran her fingers around the dotted scars that encircled her breasts.

"Anyway they're obviously doing fine," she said. "Enough of them. Tell me all about your life. We've been thrown together but we've never talked. Have some wine."

She let Chelim chat about daily life in Okré, her duties to Abeka, and other such trifles. None of it was of any interest to Krait, but she knew the maid would need to talk of familiar, comforting things before she took any risks.

It wasn't long—two cups of wine—before Chelim was sprawling on the cushions with her arms above her head, tipsy and comfortable. As Krait intended, she had talked her nerves away.

"Can I ask *you* a question?" Chelim whispered.

"It depends," Krait said.

Her loins ached. She needed to get fucked soon or she was going to lose her mind.

"What does it feel like?"

She didn't have to specify what she was talking about.

Krait rolled onto her side. She was so turned on she was getting cramps. There was no more time for cat's play.

"It can't be explained," she said. "You have to experience it. Do you want to?"

Chelim was trembling.

"A little bit. To get the idea."

"A little bit isn't good enough. I do not stop once I start, you understand? Are you up to learn what it feels like? I would like to teach you."

"Yes?" Chelim managed to squeak.

"Close your eyes."

Chelim closed her eyes, then opened them suddenly, to see what Krait was up to. Krait smiled and gently kissed her lips until her eyes were closed again.

She was done being subtle. Krait plucked Chelim's sash open, traced her hands around the contours of the maid's breasts, over her ribs, her thighs. She drew off the gossamer sleeves and kissed her elbows. At last her fingers slid down the maid's belly like a serpent, then slipped underneath her skirt.

Chelim caught her by the wrist, but didn't open her eyes. She was breathing fast.

Krait kissed her deeply until Chelim's lips parted and their tongues met, light as butterflies. The maid didn't release her grip—but made no further resistance as Krait's fingers continued down below her belly, through the soft ringlets that crowned her pudendum, and into the sea below.

Krait was so aroused she nearly orgasmed at the touch. The maid was so wet, so hot, her cunt open with desire like an orchid. Her breath came in harsh gasps and her hips writhed. Krait slipped her fingers inside and began to rock them, kneading with gentle insistence.

"Gods of all," Chelim gasped.

"Feeling good?"

"I've never felt anything so good."

"This is better."

Krait slid down the cushions. She lifted Chelim's soft thighs and parted them, cupped her rump in her palms and sank her mouth into those tender folds. She began to lap and suckle until the maid was clawing at her scalp with both hands, pushing her mouth down hard, pumping her hips.

Krait knew what she was inflicting. Chelim's senses were overwhelmed, the luscious poison of release spreading in her belly, her veins alight with holy fire.

Krait kept up the gentle torment. She felt Chelim's soft belly grow hard. The maid's face was contorted with the agony of pleasure. She hung by a single nerve on the precipice of release. Then she climaxed.

She cried out as toll after toll of savage ecstasy rang through her body.

Krait pulled herself up and they kissed until both of their faces were wet.

"*That's* what it feels like," Krait said. "But there's more you need to know."

They kissed with open mouths and dancing tongues as Krait frotted Chelim once more. She teased her nipples with teeth and tongue, nuzzled the nests of hair beneath her arms to make her ticklish, suckled the delicate skin of her sweat-slick throat. Chelim took Krait by the ears and kissed her patterned brow and cheeks, then showed her teeth and nipped Krait's lips.

The moment of dominance crumbled as pleasure took over and she was lost in it.

When Chelim came the second time, she clung desperately to Krait's neck and spasmed until she spurted into Krait's hand. After that, she had to curl up in a ball, protecting her passion-outraged cunt. She could take no more.

They drank wine and let the perspiration rise from their skins for a while.

Then, spontaneously, Chelim got onto her knees, looking down at the pirate feared by so many. The sweat-shining skin of her face and chest, stippled with concentric rings of scars in the Libagoro way, had looked so fearsome when Chelim first set eyes on her. Now they seemed to lend her vulnerability, perhaps because they pointed out the smallness of the breasts and largeness of the eyes they encircled.

Krait, lazy as a lion gorged on meat, let her stare. Chelim's eyes roamed over her body, pausing now and then on old sword cuts and lamp-soot tattoos, then following the long cords of muscle down her limbs.

She ran her hands clumsily over Krait's lean chest and belly, but didn't know quite what to do, how fast to do it, or in what order. Krait smiled and pulled her down for another thirsty kiss, then led Chelim's soft fingers to her cunt. She guided them inside of her. *Now* Chelim knew what to do, for it had just been done to her.

But she wanted to *see* Krait descend into madness. She gazed directly into the pirate's eyes and began working with her fingers, exploring, drawing them out until they pulled the hood back from her clit, then plunging them into her again.

Krait twisted her fingers into the cushions, bared her teeth in a defiant snarl, and returned Chelim's insolent stare:

"Fuck me as hard as you can."

Chelim made her come so violently that Krait jackknifed

around her hand and cried the names of the Gods, but Chelim didn't stop. The tender, frightened servant was gone, and a wicked, greedy thing had taken her place. Krait unexpectedly came again.

"Do you yield?" Chelim said, triumphantly.

"I won't yield until you fuck me to death," Krait said, and folded Chelim's dripping hand into the shape of a leaf so that her fingers were bundled together.

Then she guided her in, gasping with mingled pain and delight as those small knuckles stretched her opening to its limit, then surged deep inside.

"Now make a fist and finish me," Krait groaned through clenched teeth.

She planted her feet on the floor, thrust her hips in the air, and threw her head back. Chelim pumped relentlessly. Krait came for the third time, shouting with joy as release crashed through her body.

After that, they could only laugh, tumbled together in the sodden cushions.

"Fuck, I have to piss so bad," Krait said, once she'd caught her breath.

She dragged the chamber pot from under the bed and squatted over it. Chelim was grinning at her.

"What," Krait said.

"Can't you pee if I'm looking at you?"

Chelim also needed to relieve herself, but became shy about it once she was on the pot. Then she unexpectedly broke wind, fell over, and peed on the floor.

The two of them laughed until they wept.

Krait pulled down one of the silk curtains and draped it over the maid's shoulders, then the two of them went to the small balcony outside the floor-length window of the chamber.

They sat cross-legged in the dark, face to face, passing the flagon of herbed wine between them. They listened to the drowsy sounds of Atlantis on a humid summer night. Beyond the jumbled skyline, a three-quarter moon hung near the horizon, casting a river of dancing pearls into the sea below.

"Do you know," Chelim said, "We only met the night before this moon was born?"

"My people call that Thieve's Night," Krait said. "This is the Oasis Moon."

"What about when it's full?"

"The Shield Moon."

"I have lived in Okré for twenty years," Chelim mused, "and never set foot in your country. When I was a girl we were taught to fear the Libagoro."

"We're pretty fucking fearsome, I'm not going to lie."

"Are you afraid to die?"

"That's a heavy question."

"I had my first orgasm tonight. I'm full of heavy questions."

"For a beginner, you fucking delivered. No."

"No?"

"No, I'm not afraid to die. I'm afraid of the pain, maybe. Afraid of dying in a shameful way, or alone. But death itself doesn't frighten me."

They sat in silence for a while, pressing their feet together sole-to-sole. Then Krait spoke again.

"There's a cave in the north of my country. For thousands of years, my people have collected the right hands of our dead, wrapped them in linen, and put them in the cave. Do you know how the sashes of sailors make it home?"

"Yes. Sometimes it takes years, but many of them find their way."

"It's the same with our hands. The thing that frightens

me most is never being laid to rest there, in that cave. I haven't seen it, but it's home to all my ancestors. I'm the only pirate in the tribe, so I'll probably die at sea and be eaten by sharks. My hand will never come home."

"I thought I was going to lose my hand for a minute," Chelim said, and smiled. "Let's sleep in your bed."

31

———————

"Krait has many lovers. It could be anyone," Tar said.

"That was definitely Chelim's voice," Abeka replied.

The two of them had given up learning numbers for the day. They had climbed the stairs to the roof to escape the sounds of passion coming from the guest apartment next door.

Now they lay on cushions on the deck of the roof, drinking sweetbark brandy. It was cooler there. Hur Merker's bevy of slaves was on the lower roof of the servant's quarters at the back of the mansion, getting drunk and singing in wordless harmony.

There were voices from the roof of the mansion next door. Lanterns flickering behind the parapets all along the street told of many others having ascended to escape the indoor heat. Yet Tar and Abeka felt secret and hidden in the engulfing darkness of a tropical night. They lay close to each other but didn't dare touch.

"Chelim is allowed to have a personal life, isn't she?" Tar said.

He joined his hands behind his head, gazed up, and counted one hundred stars—because that was the highest number he'd learned so far.

Abeka spoke at last.

"What is it ordinary for two people to do?"

"When they fight?"

She rolled onto her belly and propped herself up on her elbows.

"Oh, Tar. I mean when—when they fuck."

He considered what she knew of his carnal exploits.

"You mean do people always take bizarre positions, say disgusting things, and violate each other in every way they can think of?"

"Exactly! Is it always so complicated?"

He considered this.

"No. It's best when it's not."

"Then what do they do?"

He struggled to find words. It was easier to talk of madcap sexual exploits than real love-making, which was a private thing.

"Well—Do you remember on the Barracuda on those long, warm nights, when sailors would lie with each other in the moon-shadows?"

"Yes. They would try not to cry out. I was so curious."

"That is the ordinary way. Two people giving pleasure to each other by the simplest means."

"Kissing above and below. Him inside her. Those things."

Tar had grown hard during this conversation. A bulb of desire ached in his belly.

"Yes," he muttered.

Abeka lay on her side. The firelight threw her features

into shadow, but reflected in her eyes. She was studying him, as she often did.

"Do you ever think of me in that way?"

He wasn't sure if retreating to the roof had been the best or worst idea of his life.

"I'm an escaped slave and you're the heir to the throne of the empire. Might as well be a lizard and an eagle."

"That's not an answer."

"You know the answer," he said.

Indeed, his loincloth was stretched toward the stars.

"It looks like a palace tower," she said.

"It feels like one," he groaned. "Please change the subject. Please. Anything. Let's talk about crucifixion. Skinning alive."

"Can I touch it?"

"Absolutely not."

She tentatively reached out and grasped his shaft through the fabric. Her fingers couldn't meet around it.

"It's so hot," she gasped.

"Please, oh Nameless Gods," Tar moaned, "end this jest which is my life. Destroy me. For your amusement I have suffered long enough."

"Are you praying?"

"My Gods don't respond to prayer. I'm begging."

"Can I touch it directly?"

"You'll do what you want."

By now, Tar was trembling from head to toe, his breathing labored. Abeka's soft fingers slid into his loincloth and felt the pulse beating in his outraged cock.

"It's like velvet over hot steel," she whispered.

"For the love of all Atlantis, have you lost your mind?" he choked.

He knew he was losing his own.

She laughed.

"What if I have?"

She fell across his chest and found his mouth with hers, her lips parting. When they had kissed in the street, it might have been a ploy to divert suspicion. Here, it could only be passion.

He broke away for a moment.

"Are you sure?" he whispered.

For answer she kissed him again, her hands working urgently to free their bodies of what little they wore. When at last she straddled him, they were clothed only in starlight.

She tried not to cry out.

32

Tar woke at first light. Gulls were screeching in the dim sky over the roof. Abeka slept beside him, tangled in the light coverlet under which they had nestled once their passion was spent. Hers had taken a great deal of spending, as it happened.

He studied her for a while, thinking. He could see her eyes moving behind dark-stained lids, caught in a dream of her own.

He'd been with a fair number of women, but never a princess—and certainly not *the* princess. He was doomed for this crime, of course. But all men perished. Better to die for a good reason than none. She was a very good reason.

If only she was a sailor or camel herder, they might spend their lives this way, wandering anonymously from adventure to adventure. He would like that. For the first time, he considered a future beyond the next challenge—a future lived instead of fought.

They had only just arrived, yet he felt as if they'd been stuck in Hur Merker's mansion for a year. He yearned for action, for something to do. Waiting for Rowana-Ya to sort things out did not sit well with him.

Was he an idiot to think she would not betray them? In the grand scheme of Rowana-Ya's life, he was nothing but a naughty boy she fucked from time to time. Princess Abeka was the crown jewel of the royal family. Rowana-Ya would do what she thought best, not what Tar thought best. At any moment, her private army could arrive.

And then what? Abeka would be delivered to the palace, to her mother.

He decided to take matters into his own hands.

A little while later, he descended the stairs in his traveling cloak—and was surprised to find the entire harem gathered to greet him in the foyer. Orav bowed to him.

"Good morning. You appear refreshed, Master."

"I told you before—call me Chief. Why are you all gathered here?"

He looked suspiciously about him. The seraglios appeared like the painted statues that adorned many Atlantean gardens, each in some artful pose intended to attract the eye. The effect was enhanced by the plashing fountain outside the windows, and the bright birds that flitted through the pepper trees there.

"I finally remembered where I've seen you before, Master Okré," said Orav.

"And I'm telling you, you have not," Tar replied, and marched out the door of the house.

He had no patience for this nonsense. He needed to think.

HIS THOUGHTS WERE SO CONSUMING, he found himself at the royal palace without knowing he'd arrived. He inquired of a passer-by where to find the tradesman's gate, and joined the throng gathered there.

The hood and cloak were a good disguise, as obvious as it was. He looked like every other ruffian come to the palace, hoping to develop a trade relationship with whatever minor functionary intercepted them.

He waited in a crowd of such men. There was no particular line until they got close to the portal, and then a strict pecking order was established. Woe came to the man who tried to skip ahead. After half an hour, Tar found himself near the front by discreet use of finger-holds and neck pinches.

Then he was at the gate, where the porter was writing each name in a heavy book, two burly guards glowering behind him as if looking for spelling mistakes.

"Name?"

"Hur Merker," Tar said.

This was the wrong answer. The porter looked up sharply. He squinted under Tar's hood.

"You are not Hur Merker. He needs no introduction here."

"I am his son," Tar improvised.

"He has no son."

"He has many sons, but no wives. He's on a voyage now, but I present you his mark."

Tar flashed the wax-speckled seal he'd taken from Hur Merker's desk. It bore the merchant's emblem, a shoreboat with a lion above it.

"Ah," the porter replied. "And that is why we call this the Bastard's Gate." He scribbled into the book.

Tar entered the royal palace. He breathed again for the first time in nearly a minute—he'd escaped his clumsy lie. He had not known the tradesman's entrance was called the Bastard's Gate; it was sheer luck.

There was a long, narrow corridor clad in copper beyond it. Small arched openings pierced the walls on either side, behind which were functionaries taking and giving orders for goods to the various merchants who had been permitted within. Tar continued past these, and soon entered a large hall, three balconies high, which resembled a slave auctioneer's bidding rooms.

The lowest floor, where he stood, was crowded with men like himself: common tradespeople. On the next floor were commissioners and other go-betweens, shouting out what they required. The men on the floor would bellow back with bids for the work or goods. The commissioners would point at the lowest bidders, who would then be pulled aside by a scribe in a tall, plumed hat. The two of them would sort out the details of the contract in another room devoted to the purpose.

Tar took all of this in quickly—he needed to find a way to gain entrance into the parts of the palace not served by this business. A solution presented itself to him as one of the scribes pushed past him, heading toward a man in the middle of the throng.

"I'm the one you seek," Tar said, and laid a hand on the scribe's shoulder.

It was not obvious to anyone else that he was crushing the base of the man's neck with his iron fingers. It was obvious to the scribe, however.

"As you wish," the scribe said, and accompanied Tar to the edge of the throng.

"You will go ahead of me through that door," Tar said, indicating a copper-clad arch.

The scribe did as asked, but said:

"That door leads nowhere. Only the royal provisions-rooms and the kitchens."

"I'm hungry," Tar said, and renewed his grip.

ONCE THEY WERE through the arch, Tar shifted his thumb to the scribe's superior cervical ganglion and rendered him unconscious. He dragged the senseless man behind a closet door and threw his cloak over him, then continued on his way toward the kitchens. A stairway to his left went upwards. Upwards was the direction to go if one wanted to get near the seats of power in Atlantis, so he took the stair.

It wound ever-higher, without windows or doors, until it came to a sort of interior balcony with a long drop on either hand and a doorway directly ahead. Tar set the sailor's knife in his sash for ease of drawing, then tried the handle of the door. It opened without protest. This was good, in that it meant he could continue on; it was bad, in that it meant he wasn't yet close enough to royal personages to merit keeping the doors locked.

It seemed an eternity that he wandered alone in those precincts of the palace. He did encounter servants and slaves, but they took no notice of him. He strode about as if he had lived there all his life, a trick he'd learned from Krait. Few dared question her, as she always seemed to be busy and in charge. It was hesitancy that marked a man as out of place. But in truth, his confidence was dwindling. He was completely lost.

His inner compass was unerring; he knew in which direction north lay, regardless of how many twists and turns he encountered. But north was of no use if he didn't know which way was out. He needed to find a path into the court itself, which might have been in any direction. Eventually he stopped a servant girl balancing a basket of candles on her head.

"You," he said, gruffly. "I've lost my way. Where are the queen's quarters?"

"You're in the wrong tower, Master," she said, and curtsied as much as her burden would allow. "This is the king's."

"That fool," Tar grunted. "I don't mean the king—the knave who sent me here. How do I get there?"

She considered for a moment, then said:

"Down that passage, left, then down the stairs on the right for three flights. Take the passage at the bottom to the left, then left again after the red door, up the left-hand stairs one flight. The passage on that floor only goes one way. Follow it to the livery quartermaster's stores, then make your way through that to the guardhouse. They'll check your signet, then immediate right past the laundry, left through the double arches, straight ahead to the circular courtyard with a fountain, and the queen's guardhouse is opposite."

"Thank you," Tar said, and marched onward.

He didn't understand any of what she had said after the third left, but guardhouses were no good. He decided to strike out straight across the level of the palace in which he was. As soon as he crossed a well-decorated passage, he'd take that way and risk being detained by soldiers. At least he'd be in the public parts of the palace where it was easy to get around. The parts reserved for the staff were impossible.

IN THIS MANNER he found a beautiful hallway with a wooden floor inlaid with mother-of-pearl; there he followed some elegantly-dressed courtiers until they reached a large rotunda with a domed ceiling painted like the sky. He went in the direction most people seemed to be going. Crowds were the best concealment. He soon emerged into the Royal Library.

Though he could not read, he knew what books looked like. Though he could not count, he could recognize a vast number. It seemed this place held a copy of every book in the world. Some were of thin gold sheets clapped between boards, and others were scrolls wrapped around spindles. There were accordion-folded parchments, tablets of wax and clay, and reels of cloth stitched in the same manner as sailor's sashes. Every kind of written work that human hands had invented was available in the library.

Despite the urgency of his mission, Tar could not resist gazing around him. He could almost hear those countless volumes whispering their secrets to one another. Certainly the scholars who browsed there were whispering—it was as hushed as a temple in the library, perhaps because it was difficult to read when someone was talking. His old teacher Eregin had explained that reading was a form of listening.

Half seeking a way out of the tower, and half admiring the library, Tar wandered into a light-filled room with tall windows where dozens of men and women sat apart at tables examining manuscripts, blind to the world around them.

It was there, to his surprise—although in hindsight he might have expected it—he discovered his old mate Pendrax, poring over a book.

33

"It would be best if you come with me without making a scene," Tar whispered, balancing the tip of his knife against the pulse in Pendrax's throat.

"By the mercy of Ah-Ut-Hur, I thought I'd never see you again!" Pendrax all but shouted.

Several of the nearest readers looked up with irritation, and Tar palmed his blade to keep it from view.

"That is making a scene," Tar hissed.

The doctor looked much the same as when Tar had last seen him. He wore new clothing, but his face was still sunburned, his hair lightened by the sun. A few nicks had lent his face some character.

"I'm sorry," Pendrax whispered, recovering his self-control. "I've seldom been so happy to see anyone, that's all."

"Happy to see me?" Tar grunted. "Do I kill you here, or somewhere more suitable?"

Pendrax looked genuinely amused and surprised.

"Kill me? Oh, I suppose I owe you an explanation. Let's go out onto the ramparts. I have much to tell."

The ramparts could be reached from the rotunda, Tar learned. He followed Pendrax closely with his knife poised at kidney height. The sun had crossed a quarter of the sky, but otherwise it was the same balmy day that he had left behind when he began his exploration of the palace.

He wasn't certain of the best thing to do—if he killed his enemy now, his attempt to reach the queen would have to end. He'd be forced to flee the palace. But he couldn't let the man live, or he'd certainly call the guards. It was only this dilemma that kept Pendrax alive.

For his part, Pendrax seemed at peace with the world. He stopped at an embrasure in which stood a harpoon gun large enough to sink a ship. It was not presently manned. He leaned on the low wall beneath the snout of the weapon, admiring the scene below them.

From where they stood there was a superb view of the royal harbor, where handsome ships plied the seaways or rode at anchor. Pendrax didn't seem much concerned that Tar intended to split him open.

"You look well," Pendrax smiled. "I've still got some color from the voyage, but my hands have softened up again. Right back to the sedentary life."

"Tell me why you shouldn't slip and fall over this wall," Tar said. "You have as long as it takes for that white ship to cross the harbor."

"You're upset because I shot off all those flares," Pendrax decided. "I couldn't remember which ones meant what, so I burned the lot. It worked, anyway."

"Even now the ship is halfway to the sea-gates."

"Here's the truth you wanted, and which I could not give you. I think you will understand what I have to tell you in a way that Krait Venom could not."

Pendrax turned to face him, and Tar saw no secrets in his eyes.

"I was one of a hundred men and women sent out by the king to find the princess, as soon as it was discovered she was missing from the palace at Okré. His Majesty believed her to be kidnapped."

"You are a spy?"

"I'm a doctor, as you have seen for yourself. But the king maintains a stable of folk such as I, whose work allows us to enter any place or level of society without arousing much suspicion. When called upon, we do as he bids. He bade us to find the princess. It could have been any of the others who did so, but as it happened, it was me. My theory about the priceless treasure aboard that barge proved true."

"True in a way of no value to pirates," Tar growled. "We couldn't spend a girl."

"A treasure spent is no treasure at all. I see the ship is next in line to pass into the canal, so I'll get to the point. The king saw my signal. He sailed to me straight away and I told him all that had happened. He immediately summoned the entire fleet to give pursuit. But Krait may be a genius. She escaped by going in the wrong direction, and the fleet lost the Barracuda in the very shadow of Atlantis."

"That part I know well," Tar said.

"Since then, I've been watching the king's brothers while the king himself is away playing admiral. I'm sure the princess isn't in Illusan's custody. There's been no clandestine marriage so far; the Meridian Chamber where the royals wed has been empty for months. The high priest Shadra hasn't deviated from his habits either, and the queen lurks ever in her tower."

"How do you do this watching?"

"I practice court medicine, mostly tending to noblewomen who have become pregnant while their husbands are away on voyages. All they have to do to avoid it is drink an extract of pregnant dolphin urine and abcissus leaves, but they don't like the taste and end up—"

"How is that watching?"

"These women talk. I hear everything."

"Then just say that, don't bother me with recipes for dolphin piss."

"I'm chatting with someone I consider a friend," Pendrax said, and looked hurt.

"Friends don't intend to kill you."

"My pirate friends usually do. And here we are."

Tar had no answer to that. He nodded.

"You did what you had to," he decided. "I understand that. I was going to kill you. Now I'm not sure."

"I'm glad you're having second thoughts, Chief," Pendrax

said. "Am I the villain here? The way I see it, you were going to have *some* sort of dangerous, ill-conceived adventure—no matter what. I just happened to provide you with one on behalf of the king of Atlantis."

It was Tar's turn to stare at the scenery, struggling to sort out his thoughts.

The ramparts topped a wall that stretched around the massive tower they had recently left, then curved away toward another, more slender tower decorated in silvery-white metal. There were many more towers within the walls. There were many more walls as well. This one was only half as tall as the innermost wall, but twice as tall as the outermost, which encircled the sprawling palace gardens at the foot of the towers. Even that wall was higher than a man could throw a spear.

Like Atlantis herself, the palace was a fortress within a fortress within many more.

Killing in cold blood wasn't honorable, but time ran short. Tar decided the only possible solution to his dilemma was Pendrax's death. He must find the queen before the palace was sealed for the night. Right or wrong, the man was a threat to his mission.

Then inspiration struck him: Pendrax might be of some use before he died. It might even be possible to spare his life, if things turned out right.

"You must know this palace well," Tar said.

"Better than most," Pendrax said. "Even part-time spies need to know all the ways."

"Can you get me into the queen's tower?"

"I *wondered* why you were here, but I thought it might be imprudent to ask. Yes, I can. You're looking at it, in fact."

He indicated the silvery tower along the rampart.

"Is there a way in from here?" Tar asked, eying the tower's polished metal skin.

"You might make it a few strides past the guardhouse door, but the soldiers there are better than most. Were you sent to kill her?"

Tar decided to gamble on Pendrax's sincerity.

"I come to tell the queen that the princess is alive."

Pendrax's face went bloodless under his bronzen skin. His mouth dropped open.

"Do you know where she is? At least tell me if she's here in Atlantis."

"Will you get me in front of the queen, or do I kill you and hack my way in?"

Pendrax tugged at his earlobe and studied Tar's face as he would a patient's. Tar suspected the man was trying to decide how much to trust him. In that respect, their thoughts were moving in the same direction.

"I don't question your motives," Pendrax said. "But I have reason to believe the queen may not be... the ideal recipient of word from the princess. I can't say more."

"You're going to have to say more," Tar replied, closing in eye-to-eye, his hand falling to the hilt of his knife.

Pendrax stared back defiantly.

"You're never diplomatic, yet often persuasive, Tar Yunkai. I'll tell you something more, and if it's not enough, kill me on the spot. You'll get nothing else from me."

Although they were alone on the rampart, Pendrax leaned even closer to Tar and spoke in a whisper. What he had to say could reach no other ears.

"The king speaks to me in confidence sometimes, ever since you and I parted ways. The doctors here are all spies for someone or other—I happen to be his. He can't even trust his *own* doctor, who is my master. He can seek my advice without his concerns being relayed straight to some scheming enemy."

"Tell me the secret, not the story about the secret."

"It's not easy. I haven't told anyone else about this."

"Get on with it or I will throw you off the wall. You have until the count of three."

Pendrax was surprised.

"Did you learn how to count?"

"I know three, so you'd better get on with it."

"His Majesty thinks the queen is insane."

OF ALL THE things Pendrax could have said, this was the only one that threw Tar's plans into ruin.

If the queen had gone mad, she would be of no use protecting Abeka from her scheming brother-in-law and whoever wanted her dead.

Tar swore and stamped across the rampart until he'd mastered his fury enough not to kill Pendrax out of frustration alone. Then he clamped his hard fingers on the doctor's shoulder.

"You're no friend of mine, Pendrax—but you're no enemy, either. Today you live. Get me out of this accursed palace by the swiftest way you know. I'll bring word to the princess of her mother's condition."

"Tell her to be safe, most of all," Pendrax said. "That is the king's only wish."

"Hippo shit. She says her father hates her."

"That's because she has a child's understanding of why she was sent away. The king loves her deeply—he didn't banish her all the way to Okré as punishment. He put her there to keep her safe from enemies in the Atlantean court."

"How do I convince her this is true?"

"Think about it, Tar. You're ignorant, not stupid. Is her life safe here?"

"No."

"Was it safe in Okré?"

"It was. I see your point. Take me out of here. There's no time to waste."

34

Pendrax was a better spy than Tar gave him credit for. He had gleaned that the princess was almost certainly in Atlantis. In addition, he had a few operatives of his own.

Once he'd taken Tar down through a series of disused ways and concealed doors to a postern gate in the outermost wall, he signaled to one of these confederates, a woman who sold spicy dried fish from a handcart near that very gate.

"Follow that swordsman," he said to her. "Don't let him see you. Report back to me the moment you see him go into an inn or private house."

She wheeled her cart into the crowded street and was soon gone from Pendrax's sight. Tar was visible for longer—wherever he went, people got out of his way.

Tar, aware he was likely to be followed, took a meandering route back to the old Captain's Quarter of the city. He stopped for a bitter sea-grass beer in a small tavern, idled a while to watch a game of bounders played by some apprentices in the street, and studied the wares in a chandlery, although he had little present interest in ropes or canvas.

At each of these stops, he took in the faces around him. Did anyone look familiar? Was anyone watching him, or pointedly *not* watching him? Either of those was suspicious. Rowana-Ya had told him about such things, given all the spies at court—and the ever-present threat of kidnapping for ransom.

Tar didn't see anyone behaving oddly, nor did he recognize any faces he'd seen before. He relaxed and let his thoughts turn again to what Pendrax had said.

He was convinced the man had told the truth about the king. To Abeka the child, being sent away into her nasty uncle's care so far from home must have seemed like an act of hatred.

Abeka the adult had no new information to alter her view —she'd mentioned her father regularly wrote letters to her, and that they contained mostly trivia and superficial descriptions of events in the capitol. She felt he was taunting her with news of the life he had denied her at the Atlantean Court.

But the king had sent the entire fleet to save his daughter —as many ships as there were leaves in a forest. That was an act of love, not hatred or indifference. Tar understood this now.

And Pendrax had said the king thought the queen was insane. Tar believed him, because he nearly had to throw the doctor off the palace wall to get him to admit it.

So the person he should take Abeka to was not the queen. It was the *king*. But the king was out on the sea somewhere, which meant his brothers could act unopposed. Tar was back where he started: the only person between Abeka and her enemies was himself.

These thoughts were like a storm cloud that dimmed the

busy streets around him. He could hear a bumping sound like a slave's oar that reminded him the price of keeping Abeka alive and free was most likely his own life and freedom. Yet for some reason, he was prepared to pay it.

That bumping sound, though—he'd been hearing it for a long time, and hadn't noticed until now. It wasn't an oarlock, of course. He was far from any shipping. What was it?

He stopped in his tracks and turned back to admire a prostitute who had offered him a free half-hour if he'd pay for an hour. He'd never yet had to pay for a woman's time, nor had he any inclination to do so, but it gave him an opportunity to study the crowd behind her.

That thumping sound was either a wooden leg or a wheel, he thought. That was when he saw the woman with a handcart laden with dry, spiced fish. She was bent nearly double to push the cart, so she was usually hidden by the crowd. The cart had a cracked wheel.

Tar's eyes narrowed. The spot to sell such wares was near the canals. She was in the wrong place. And she was looking everywhere but at him.

Tar turned his attention to the prostitute. She was bonny enough, not too young nor old, with long copper-dusted breasts that pushed down her girdle in front, and a broad rump that lifted it up behind. Her eyes were fixed with great interest on his breechclout.

"Another day," he said, and put a pair of copper crabs in her palm. "Drink a dram for me."

He ambled onward, ignoring the offer of a free hour if he paid for half an hour. At the next intersection, he turned down a narrow alley.

When he emerged at the far end, the woman with the cart was no longer following him. He hadn't killed her, but she would regret her meddling when she regained consciousness.

He gnawed on a piece of peppery fish and pondered his dilemma, and by a looping, haphazard path, eventually returned to the house of Hur Merker.

There was an ambush waiting behind the door.

35

When Tar returned, mind still sunken in thought, he found himself confronted with the nine women of his host's harem. They surrounded him and fell into seductive poses. His way upstairs was blocked.

Orav circled him like a cat with its prey, drawing nearer and nearer. He could smell the perfumed oil in her hair. He began to perspire.

"You are the Golden Prince. I have watched you fight a hundred times," she said. "I should have guessed it sooner, but all Atlantis thought you were dead."

"We have all seen your prowess," said Jinneh, the smallest of the harem. She was the same age as the rest, but as petite as a child, with breasts the size of oranges.

"Our master Hur Merker sends us out with his guests who want to see the arena," Orav explained. "It's dreary watching people die, but we were thrilled to watch you live."

"I don't know what you're talking about," Tar snarled. Real anger was rising in him.

Now Orav was close enough to lick his lips, if she wished.

When she spoke, her breath was in his nostrils. He caught the scent of cloves and sweet wine.

"You do, Golden Prince. I even remember when you got this scar."

She ran her fingertip along his pectoral muscle and made it jump.

"All of us used to talk about you after the fights. How we wanted to bathe your aching limbs and tend to your wounds."

"And massage the knots from your muscles," said golden-skinned Ki-Ya, whose back was patterned in blue.

"And suck your cock," said bold Apal-Opa, who was the tallest, as slender as a wading-bird.

The other women laughed like little bells and pretended to be shocked. Several hands fell upon his skin, as if to reassure him, and then began to glide, lightly as moth-wings.

"By the Gods, what is this game?"

Tar was infuriated and confused. And highly aroused.

"We mustn't frighten him," said Orav. "Come take a cushion, Chief, and let us assuage your fears."

Tar found himself propelled into the cool entertaining-room like a feather borne on the lightest breeze. These women had joined together against him, yet he could not find the will to resist. They had him reclining on a couch, his sandals off and a cup of wine in his hand, before he could even recall why he must say no.

"I do not confess to be this prince," he said, "but I have been a slave myself. I am a free man now. I will not take a woman who is not free. She has no will of her own."

"If we had our own free will, every one of us would lie with you as greedily as suckling piglets at the teat, Golden Prince."

"But you do not have free will. She who can't say no, therefore can't say yes."

"You're the worst master in the world," said Ditula, the plumpest of the girls. She stamped her naked foot so that her flesh jiggled, sending an urgent spark of desire into Tar's guts.

The others nodded in agreement and pouted at Tar.

Orav went on: "We asked your slave girl if someone had wounded your member during a fight. She said it was nothing to do with that. She admitted she'd seen you grow hard in her presence, and caught you studying her backside—although she would rather die than have you know this. She said you are the most decent-minded man alive, when you're not butchering your foes."

"Don't tell me this!" Tar barked. "You are betraying her secret." He buried his face in the wine to hide his desperate confusion.

"Once we knew you were still virile, but all wrapped up in your sense of honor," Orav breathed, "we made a deal among ourselves."

She looked about at the other women. They nodded.

"We agreed upon a plan, because we knew you'd say no, even if it made your great big balls turn blue."

Orav sat on the couch so that her warm silk-clad haunches nestled against his thighs.

"Our real master, you see, is as impotent as a cup of milk. He gets his delights from being intolerable. It's all he can muster. And most of his guests aren't much better—or they're worse, in their own ways. We're desperate women, as you can imagine. We pleasure each other, of course, but there's no substitute for an iron-hard cock with a lusty man behind it."

"I'd free you if I could," Tar said. "And then we would fuck like beasts. But I have no such power."

Rea, the forest woman with long, sharp canines and eyes like a fox, refilled his cup from behind him. Her nipples tautened against his skin. He shivered involuntarily. His cock, which lacked any moral compass, was so erect it was pulling his loin-clout away from his sash.

"Here's what we can do, my Prince," Orav said. "If we can't say yes, what if you don't say no?"

His mind was whirling.

"I don't understand."

"You do whatever I say, and I do whatever I want. No matter what it is, you have to go along with it. This one time, I am the master. If you do not agree to this, then you are as bad as all the rest, denying a slave girl her wish as only a slave-master can."

Tar couldn't frame an argument against the idea. He could hardly frame a thought at all. His furiously beating heart had found its way into his groin.

"Take off your clothes," Orav said, her voice sharp and commanding, all the honey gone. "Do it now."

TAR ROSE TO HIS FEET, meaning to flee to the room. But his feet wouldn't move. The women drew off his borrowed sleeves and untied his sash. They pulled the tuck out of his loincloth, and let it fall to the floor. He was naked, his cock jutting out like the polished figurehead of a ship. He could feel the nine pairs of eyes roaming over his body as much as if they touched him.

"These others will pleasure each other. You will pleasure me," Orav said. "Fetch the oil and water, Apal-Opa."

THEY BATHED him with their eighteen hands and ninety fingers and it was all Tar could do not to spend his burden in the first half-minute. He ground his teeth together. Then they laved his skin with the oil, and a pearl formed on the tip of his aching cock.

"Turn away," Orav demanded. He did.

She pressed herself against his back and sucked his earlobe into her mouth. One oily hand was splayed against his quivering belly. She slid the other into the cleft of his buttocks.

"Don't you dare resist," she snarled into his ear, when he clenched his muscles against her questing fingers. "Don't you fucking dare."

With that, she stroked his asshole and cock at the same time, then entered him with her fingers, pushing deep, and massaged his prostate until he came so hard he cried out like an animal and spattered the floor. The other women, who had been falling into writhing twos and threes around them, cooed with delight.

"If you go soft I'll cut it off," Orav said. "Rea and Uakatu, lift me up and slide that serpent into me before I die of desire. There has been a change of plans, little man. You're going to fuck us all."

Tar did as he was told.

36

Krait and Chelim were in the guest quarters next door to Hur Merker's chambers.

"Whatever is happening over there?" Chelim whispered.

"Sounds to me like Master Tar is getting his money's worth out of those slaves," Krait said. "We should take a bath together to cement our companionship."

"We are perfectly unsuitable companions," Chelim said.

"Nah. Princess Abeka and Tar Yunkai are perfectly unsuitable. She's pretending to be a slave and he's pretending to be a human being. I'd love to know how that's going. You and me, we just need to learn how to get along."

"I'm so worried for her," Chelim sighed.

"Don't fret. Tar's got the brains of a starfish, but he'll never take advantage of her."

"It's not him I'm worried about. She... Well, she couldn't stop talking about him during our voyage to Atlantis."

Krait chuckled. "She *complained* about him the whole time. Criticizing Tar is something we have in common."

Chelim shook her head.

"You know nothing of her world. When a high-born woman is interested in a man, that's what she does. She criticizes him bitterly. The more bitterly, the more interested she is."

"Idiots. Tell me how you got the job of being her maid. Did they pick you out of a lineup, or did you have to pass a test?"

"Princess Abeka asked for me. It was the greatest honor of my life. My mother was a linens-maid in the Okrean palace, you see, and as a girl I often went with her to help clothe the beds. One day, we found a weeping child in the darkest corner of a bedroom that had been empty the day before."

"Abeka, of course."

"At the time, we didn't know who she was. I was moved by pity to ask why she sorrowed. She told me she had been sent away from her family. I didn't know she was a princess —let alone *the* princess—or I'd have been too afraid to talk to her. But we became friends, if I may be so bold as to claim such a status."

Krait, who had only been half-listening, said:

"She's seen his famous dong. That's gotta be weird. Do you think they got it on, yet?"

Chelim was outraged, both for Abeka's dignity and for not being listened to.

"That's hardly any of your business! Are you suggesting they might...*couple*?"

Cries of ecstasy rang through the mansion. Krait laughed.

"After what's happening to him right now, I doubt he'll be able to. Don't you worry about the princess' honor. Tar is too irritatingly decent-minded to make a move on his own, and I doubt she's going to open her knees for a fugitive slave."

"The very thought of it is appalling. Never speak of this again."

"No," Krait said, adopting her sexiest pose, "the person you need to worry about in terms of seduction is yourself—because you find me irresistible."

"It's true," Chelim sighed.

"Look, if listening to the athletics downstairs gives you nerves, let's do some reconnaissance instead. We have to be ready to split at a moment's notice if things go sideways. Let's scope out a ship to steal."

THREE BRONZE SERPENTS LATER—THE price of a private sailboat on the Summer Canal—they were looking out at the teeming Great East Harbor on the edge of Atlantis. A thousand ships and boats of every description were moored there, and nearly as many plied the water to and from the sea beyond. Sails were as numerous and bright as feathers on a bird, and banks of oars undulated along copper and wooden hulls like the legs of millipedes.

"Every one a voyage. I want to sail them all," Krait said.

She was truly a daughter of the sea. The mere sight of the water and the vessels upon it was enough to flood her spirit with courage.

"What are we looking for?" Chelim asked.

To her, all ships and boats were alike. Some larger, some smaller, but otherwise the same.

"That one," Krait said.

She pointed out a ship moored mid-harbor. Its hull was painted sky blue and its furled sails were dyed orange.

"What makes it suitable?"

"Her make, for one thing. She's a gaff cutter. See her mast is boomed aft, she's rigged for three headsails, and she's got that long, gaff-rigged bowsprit? And her hull—broad beam, steep deadrise, high prow, and no ass to speak of. She's built to go like a bat out of hell, and nothing else.

Perfect escape craft. And I like that blue paint. Are you listening to me?"

Chelim was not.

"No hard feelings," Krait concluded. "I don't listen to you either."

Krait and Chelim returned to Hur Merker's mansion to find Tar in the reception room, brooding. Several of the harem-women were lurking about. He ignored them.

"You look like a hernia," Krait observed.

"I don't understand the caste thing," Tar grumbled.

"Did your slave give you a hard time? Fucking slap her, Chief. Anyway, where is she?"

"Upstairs, I think," Tar said.

"Hey slave," Krait said to Apal-Opa, "Fetch that haughty bitch of his."

Chelim was outraged. Krait placed a silencing finger on her lips. Apal-Opa went upstairs.

"I found a seaworthy tub we can steal if we need to make a hasty exit," Krait said to Tar. "Where were you this morning?"

"Advance scouting," Tar said. "Route to the palace."

"She isn't upstairs, Chief," Apal-Opa called from the top of the stairs.

Tar's instincts prickled an alarm.

"Has anyone seen her?" he barked.

"Not since before we... dallied with you, Chief."

"Nobody else? By the Gods," Tar said, and rushed for the door.

"You want backup?" Krait asked.

"Search the house and grounds. I'll head for the canal. It's the only place she knows."

37

An hour later, Tar had patrolled the route by which they'd come to the Old Captain's Quarter, and all the streets that crossed it. He'd been up and down the canal on both sides. He knew the chances of finding Abeka were few—if she had stepped into a shop along the way, he could have missed her. Besides, he had only searched the surface level deck, where the sun fell. There were countless streets below his feet, twisting through the shadowy guts of Atlantis.

It was futile. She was probably hiding in the mansion, in which case he'd wasted his time for nothing. The princess confused him. She teased him, defied him, and yet seemed to value his company. She was clever and sensible, but at the same time irresponsible. He wondered if he could ever understand.

As he pondered the nature of princesses, his eyes wandered over the busy avenue alongside the canal. He would turn into the quarter at the next intersection. When he looked in that direction, he saw a familiar figure concealed in a hooded cloak, waiting to cross while a team of camels passed by. The regal posture was unmistakable.

"Do you know how easy it was to surprise you?" Tar hissed, catching her elbow from behind.

Abeka gasped. "Where did you come from?"

"The same place the assassin who kills you will come from."

She pulled her hood tight. "I was stupid."

"Yes, you were."

"I'm sorry.

"I don't care."

He took her roughly by the wrist. When she began to protest, he tightened his grip. He knew it hurt. He needed it to hurt. His fingers closed like iron hinges.

She cried out in pain.

He saw real fear in her face.

He let go.

"You think that hurts?" he said. "Now imagine a knife in your kidneys. People have already died trying to get to you. I can't stop them all."

She kneaded her wrist.

"I understand."

"*That* is what I wanted to hear, not 'sorry'. Of course you're sorry. You take responsibility for your actions. What I'm worried about is you don't seem to get the seriousness of the situation."

"Let's go back. People are looking at us."

Tar glared around at the curious bystanders. A troop of soldiers was marching toward them. She was right—they had made themselves conspicuous. He wanted to draw his weapon and fight them all.

The soldiers were almost upon them, and their captain had observed Tar's scowl in his direction.

"I'm tired of hiding," he growled. "I'm tired of pretending."

"So am I," said Abeka.

She took his face in her hands and kissed him.

It was the perfect subterfuge. To everyone around, the quarrel immediately made sense. *It was just one of those lovers' things. Look at them kissing. Nothing spices love better than an argument.*

There were countless mismatched couples in Atlantis. The place thrived on impossible romances. These two were an ordinary sight.

The soldiers marched past.

When at last their mouths parted, they stared into each other's eyes in a state of mutual shock. They had done this before, but alone, in secret, and wild with lust. This was different. It felt like an announcement—of something they both wanted the world to know.

"What the frozen hell was that?" Tar said.

"We had better get back to the house. I promise you I won't leave the premises again until we depart for good."

They walked in silence for a while. Tar could hardly form thoughts.

"May I speak freely... Master?" Abeka said.

"What."

"Where did you go today, before you were ambushed by the harem?"

"How much of that did you see?"

"Answer my question."

"I went somewhere entirely for my own good, and none of yours," he admitted. "You would hate me for it."

"A bawdy house? The arena, to watch a fight from the

other side of the sand? Where could you possibly have gone that would disappoint me?"

"It's not worth the telling."

She stopped and placed her hands on his shoulders. This fearless man, who thought nothing of a brutal death if it served some small purpose, was afraid she would be upset with him.

Impulsively, she hugged him to her bosom, her arms wrapped around his head, her fingers tangled in his sailor's knotted hair. She wanted him to feel safe with her. She felt a desperation she could not name.

"Where did you go?" she repeated, her lips pressed to his collarbone. "Just tell me. Please tell me, if it troubles you so."

He gently unraveled her grasp. He took her hands and looked into her eyes with sorrow.

"I went to tell your mother where you are."

38

———

Abeka ran.

Tar couldn't catch up with her until she was out of breath—she ducked and dodged nimbly through the crowds, while he plowed along like a fork-nosed rhino. At last, he caught her by the wrist and pulled her into a recessed doorway that provided some shelter.

"Will you never listen? Your enemies are everywhere!" he hissed.

"My enemy holds me now against my will," she replied, showing her teeth.

He let go of her arm, but blocked her escape.

"I didn't speak to her," he said. "But I found one we both know, and he revealed important things—things you should be aware of. I came back to tell you, but was distracted by those women. They do not take 'no' for an answer."

"I don't care whether you spoke to her, I'm angry that you tried to do it. Why would you turn me over to my family? You know my uncle will marry me the instant I am found. Why would you wish that upon me?"

"Let's argue at Hur Merker's place, not here."

"I won't be humiliated in front of those women," she said. "They know I'm a spoiled fool."

A rare moment of clarity struck him.

"You're jealous! I fucked them and it upset you. That's why you went out!"

"Why would I be jealous? You're a murderous, lowborn barbarian."

"That's exactly why women like me."

He thought she might try to escape again, so he threw his heavy arm around her shoulders and laughed as if he hadn't a care in the world.

He added an urgent whisper: "We can't stay in the street chatting like fools. That cloak of yours is a thin disguise. We'll talk in that tavern, where I can fight with my back to a wall."

THEY SAT in a dim corner near the rear entrance. The place was thick with the cold smell of oxidized copper and seagrass beer.

"I don't know how you resisted the urge to kill Pendrax," Abeka said, when Tar finished his full telling of the day's adventure.

"The healer's not the sort of man I judged him to be," he said, and drank half of his mug in one go.

"How can he be so sure my father doesn't hate me? He doesn't know either of us well enough for that."

"Think of what your father did from the standpoint of a grown woman, rather than the child you were. It all makes sense. Even those letters he writes you—would he dare fill them with personal details and fatherly tenderness? Of course not. He knows his enemies intercept them, looking for weakness. What he writes can't betray affection, or his affection will betray him. I believe what Pendrax told me."

"I would like to believe it," she said to her cup of biridi.

This was another taste she had developed at sea. Nobody in the royal court would drink such low-class alcohol—but that wasn't entirely true. There was one other.

She smiled for the first time in an hour.

"I imagine my father likes biridi, don't you?"

"He's a seaman. I'm sure he does."

"We have that in common."

"And other things. I'd say you get your courage from him —and your nose, if the portraits in the palace are accurate."

"It amazes me that you have been there more recently than I. Is it splendid?"

"If you like that kind of thing. It's like a treasure box made of treasure."

"How I would like to live there again," she said, and swallowed the last of the liquor.

She exhaled with an 'aaah', as nearly everyone did. It was necessary to let the fire out of the lungs. Tar was staring at her as if she'd sprouted gills.

"Why are you gaping at me?" she asked, and burped. Her ancestors would be appalled.

"You just found the answer to our problem. I've been distracted, and that's always when the solution appears, isn't it?"

"You know how to keep me safe—and single?"

He thumped his points out on the table with a fingertip.

"There are ten thousand young women at the palace. I saw them everywhere. Hardly a soul knows what you look like fully grown; your portraits in Atlantis are all out-of-date. Instead of hiding in the public eye, you should be hiding in the palace."

"Doing what?"

"I don't know. Beg for a job. Sew sleeves or fetch water. Pretend to be a common maid like Chelim. Only until your father returns, which could be any day now. Then you can reveal yourself, and become the princess again under your father's protection."

"It's a mad idea, but the best one we have," she said.

Tar finished his beer and rotated the froth-rimed mug between his hands.

"There's something else on your mind," she said, when the pause grew long.

Tar scratched the stubble on his chin. He rubbed his leather-hard palms on his thighs. He was nervous. She had seen him in many moods, but never nervous.

At last he spoke.

"Why am I not good enough for a princess? Because of my caste? It's stupid. I get jealous, too. "

"I didn't say I was jealous."

"But were you?"

"Yes."

He stared at her with his desert-colored eyes, searching for words.

"There's a song that says jealousy is the shadow cast by love. Is that true? What is love? I can't understand my feelings for you."

She blushed so furiously it was as if her skin had been scalded. But he clearly expected an answer, so she mastered her confusion.

"I asked my nursemaid the same thing, once," Abeka said. "She told me love was like an unquenchable thirst."

"A thirst for someone else?"

"That's how she saw it. For myself—I don't know. I went mad over boys for a while, when I was new to the idea of them. But that was different. I was making up fantasies about pretty fellows who turned out to be otherwise dull and ordinary."

"I am not a pretty fellow."

"Nor dull and ordinary. What do *you* think love is?"

Tar rubbed the back of his neck.

"My people are not loving. They fight and survive. In the fighting-pits I was taught that love is a weakness. But Motia —my mate in the pits—she knew what it was. She told me she loved me, and then she died. I am very far from understanding it."

"How did *you* feel about *her?*"

"She never told me."

Abeka sighed deeply.

"Witness the Gods, you have been cruelly broken, Tar Yunkai."

She was sad now. Tar regretted talking about it.

"Here's what I know," he said. "I was ready to die for her freedom. I'm ready to die for yours."

He looked closely at her. Damp lashes veiled her downcast eyes. A pair of fine parenthetical lines framed her mouth. The thin scar on her throat danced to her pulse.

She almost spoke several times before she said, "It could be you're in love."

He might have said almost anything else and gotten away with it, but he said:

"That seems unlikely."

Sudden anger overtook her. She stood up, stiff as a soldier.

"Will you stop saying horrible things, please?"

"All I said was—"

She pointed a quaking finger at his face.

"The real problem with you is you're afraid to love anyone —because you lack the courage to lose them."

His face was stone.

"I apologize," she said. "That was a very harsh thing to say."

He rose and scattered coins on the table.

"What difference does it make? Apparently, I lack the courage to care."

39

Tar was prepared for an attack—but not from *inside* the compound.

He'd gotten Abeka back without incident, on high alert every step of the way. It was a great relief when they reached the mansion. She was safe again, or so he imagined.

But as they came to Hur Merker's gate, a swarm of armed men poured out of the opening, surrounding them. Tar reached for his knife, and his fist closed on nothing. He'd left it in the mansion in his rush to find Abeka.

"Give up the woman and live," their leader lied.

Tar assessed the situation. The attackers were mercenaries working for a contractor; their equipment was all from the same source. They wore studded leather girdles, iron caps, and scarves wrapped around their faces. Every man carried his weapon of choice. Two hands of men—ten, he'd learned—and there was another at each end of the street, keeping watch. Twelve, that was.

Tar liked hawk-axes, so he attacked the man who brandished one.

They hadn't expected such an immediate response, and they hadn't expected him to start the fight.

His fist sank into the man's face and the hawk-axe was his, but a short spear found his flesh before he could bring it to bear. The point skidded off his shoulder blade or he'd have been dead. These men were skilled and fearless.

Tar had been forced to leave the relative safety of the gate arch to arm himself, so he was fighting men on all sides. In such situations, the best defense was to continuously change height and direction—crouching, leaping, rolling and rising, always turning—which was exhausting, even if he had been fresh.

He cut a man's kneecap free of its moorings and parted another from the majority of his right arm, but with every victory they got a piece of him in return. A few more stabs and cuts and he'd have bled too much to keep fighting.

He didn't spare any attention for Abeka. She wasn't stupid. She could flee or be captured—that was her decision to make. But when he heard a woman scream behind him and a man's severed head flew past his own, he had to see what was going on.

The scream was Krait's. With a savage grin she leaped over the headless body into the fray, and her red sword flew like a flame among the mercenaries, ripping them apart. Chelim was behind her, pulling Abeka into the courtyard. The gate slammed shut after them.

Tar's bloodlust was renewed. The man who managed to pierce his leg with a trident took the axe under his chin, then Tar wrenched the barbed spear out of his flesh and threw the weapon at the leader of the mercenaries. Of the three points, two found eye sockets.

The remaining men fled the moment their commander hit the deck. One collapsed before he reached the corner. His mates dragged him away, painting a bloody smear down the street.

"When did you start to suck at fighting?" Krait laughed, looking at Tar's ragged wounds.

He spat on the ground.

"This was my second battle of the day."

THEY TUMBLED into the house and bolted the door. Krait bellowed orders to the seraglios. They did exactly as she said, locking all the window shutters and checking that the hatches and passages below street level were secure. Their habitual, playful insolence was gone. They had reason to be terrified.

The mercenaries had arrived almost as soon as Tar had left to find Abeka. They made it quite clear what was going to happen once they had the girl of interest in their custody—the client had told them to kill the master of the house and seize the slave with him. What they did with the remaining slaves was of no importance.

While they waited for their targets to return, the killers had outlined their plans for the harem in such detail that Ditula had to be restrained from cutting her own wrists.

While the slaves rushed about the place closing it up, Krait, Tar, and Abeka could speak without fear of being overheard. As they did so, Abeka and Chelim wrapped up the worst of Tar's wounds.

Krait was in her usual high spirits, and unharmed.

"I guess we're done sitting around with our thumbs up our asses," she said. "Looks like it's time to move out of here."

"Earlier, somebody tried to follow me," Tar said. "I put a stop to it. But based on what just happened, somebody else succeeded. Have you been careful?"

Krait spat on the floor. "Blow it out your ass, you prick. I've been the fucking soul of discretion."

"You did get drunk with Skraj and that sailor with no front teeth," Chelim pointed out.

"You treacherous, two-faced, tattle-tale bitch," Krait replied, affectionately. "Fut-Ye and Skraj would never betray me."

Chelim had learned some defiance over the course of her adventures. She refused to back down.

"That doesn't mean you weren't overheard. I warned you!"

"Hey, *he's* the one who got followed. I'm guessing he fucked up. Did you fuck up? Please tell me you fucked up."

"I did fuck up," Tar said. "I talked to somebody as well."

"This person got a name?"

"We can get into that later. Abeka and I discussed it, and we think the safest place for her now is in the royal palace."

"That's a shitty plan. If she shows up there, she's getting married to His Highness Duke Niecefucker within the hour."

Abeka didn't like to be discussed in the third person when she was right there.

"I'm going to pretend to be a palace servant until my father returns. Then it will be safe to reveal myself."

Chelim was scandalized.

"You can't do that! It's bad enough pretending to a slave here in this small household, but if you—at the royal court— No. I won't allow it. It would be the scandal of the century."

"They almost got me, Chelim. Their bodies yet lie in the street outside. Nowhere is safe. Nowhere but the palace."

"Then what do *I* do?"

Chelim's greatest fear was coming true. She would have to leave Abeka's side.

"If it's acceptable to her, you'll stay with Krait until things are sorted out," Abeka said.

"Fucking yes," Krait said, and pumped her fist.

"That's enough doctoring," Tar said to the women. "The rest of these are only scratches."

"I can see bone at the bottom of this one," Abeka pointed out.

Tar stood up. "The bone is only scratched. We have to get out of here now. Leave everything behind. We're going straight to the palace. Orav!"

The slave paused—she'd been running past to go upstairs. "Yes, Prince?"

"Don't call me that. I need you to go to Lady Mannon's palace straight away. Tell her what happened, and to send her personal army back here to get the rest of you out."

"I will, Tar Yunkai."

"Anybody coming out of that gate is a target, so bring your colleague with the muscles—Uakatu—and be ready for a scuffle. If you see anyone following you, run for it, but word *must* get through or you could all die."

"Uakatu!" Orav shouted up the stairs.

The dancer came bounding down, beads of sweat standing out on her bald head.

"We have an urgent mission. We must go this instant."

"What kind of urgent mission?" Uakatu asked. She was as bewildered by the sudden change of atmosphere as everyone else.

"This kind of urgent," Krait said, and handed over her knife. "You know how to use one of these? Insert it in anybody who tries to fuck with you."

Uakatu touched the flat of the blade to her forehead—a good sign. That was a fighter's gesture.

"Please tell the others to be silent and stay locked up until help arrives," Orav said to the group in general.

Then she unbolted the front door. The courtyard was empty. Uakatu preceded her to check that the street was clear. Nobody was looking her way; the spectacle of dead and wounded drew every eye. Before she left, Orav turned back and locked eyes with Tar.

"Die with a red blade, Golden Prince," she said, and was gone.

40

———

The fugitives had made most of the distance to the palace—they could see the sail of the King's Tower over the rooftops—when Abeka's enemies struck again.

Chelim, Abeka, Tar, and Krait were in the street, fully armed, cloaks thrown carelessly over their heads. Chelim insisted that she and Abeka switch clothing, which they did in the courtyard. If anyone was to be captured, better if they got the wrong woman first.

So the party hurried along. They gave up trying to be inconspicuous. There was no point blending in if their opponents were on the alert. They pushed through the crowds, dashed in front of camel-wagons, and leaped across narrow canals rather than seek out a footbridge.

Their path led straight to the heart of Atlantis without any of the now-customary twists and turns. When the mast of the royal palace came into view, Tar bade them stop a moment. He was dizzy from loss of blood.

"From here on is where the greatest danger lies," he said. "This is where our enemies' power is concentrated. If we have to cut our way to the front gate, that's what we'll do. But whatever happens to the rest of us—Abeka, you must get inside."

"There's too much blood on my hands as it is," she replied. "If I give myself up, maybe we can avoid—"

"Get over it," Krait said. "A shit-ton of people will die in your name before you get old, Princess. That's just how it goes for you royal types."

Chelim, gasping for breath, raised a hand in protest.

"Don't die, Krait," she said. "You told me we could go sailing again soon."

Krait gallantly kissed Chelim's knuckles.

"You know it, Baby. All I ask is if I die between here and that palace, raise a fucking statue of a huge-ass, solid gold buffalo right where I fall. And make sure my name's on it in big letters. You picking up what I'm putting down, Princess?"

"I am, Captain Krait Venom Libagoro of Men. What of you, Tar Yunkai?"

Tar found the box of jabbo tucked into his sash. For the first time, he snorted up a quantity of the powder. It struck his nose like lightning. He felt as vigorous as if he'd risen from a restful sleep.

"I have no intention of dying today," he said, and drew his sword.

They plunged into the web of streets that ringed the palaces, running at full tilt.

THE ENEMY'S plan to capture the princess alive was no longer in effect. The fugitives had to cross a small square surrounding one of the countless statues of heroes and gods with which Atlantis was decorated. They hadn't gone more than five strides into the open space when there came the metallic hammer-blow sound of a harpoon springbow launching its missile.

Chelim was dead before she knew she was hurt. The harpoon passed through her heart and lungs, pulling the princess' cloak all the way through with it. She dropped headlong to the deck of the square and blood poured steadily from her as from a spilled wine-jug—there was no heartbeat to make it jump.

Abeka screamed, and couldn't stop screaming.

The shot had come from the flat roof of one of the mock-palatial houses in that district.

Krait saw the attacker first—a man struggling to reload the ungainly weapon from behind an ornamental parapet.

"The Barracuda for a fucking bow!" she shouted. "Tar, go the fuck on. I've got work to do."

With that, ignoring Tar's demand that she stay with the group, Krait was across the square and vaulting over the front garden wall of the house.

"Abeka, we can't stay," Tar said, and pulled her up from Chelim's crumpled body.

He had to drag her to cover on the opposite side of the square—and there met two swordsmen, who had guessed the wrong woman lay dead. They were quick and tough, but they had never met an opponent who moved as fast as Tar. His sword seemed to vanish when it struck the first man across the face, then reappeared in the breast of the second. An instant later it sprang out of the back of the first man.

Tar didn't waste the seconds it would take to pull his sword out, but caught that man's weapon as it fell from his grasp. Then he was dashing down the street again, towing Abeka behind him. He hadn't let go of her hand during the entire skirmish.

The next man came at them from a doorway, and his momentum kept him running across the street until his guts tangled around his knees and he fell on his face, heaving up blood.

They came to a spacious avenue with narrow parks running along the roadway, at the far side of which was a wide bridge that reached the palace district. Rowana-Ya's palace was on the far side of the royal grounds. On this side were embassies.

Sightseers were strolling about, rich slave-borne palanquins going to and fro. Beautifully-armored soldiers were marching in perfect order, and canal boats drifted over the water, packed with commuters and tourists.

The fugitive pair ran straight for the nearest bridge, careless of the spectacle they must have been. In moments, a squad of soldiers was going after them—but the men threw themselves down when another harpoon slammed into a tree near Abeka.

The shaft pierced the trunk through-and-through. Now the soldiers' attention was on finding the source of the missile, not the bloodied pair fleeing it.

In moments, Tar and Abeka were across the bridge.

41

The nearest gate to the Royal Palace, known as the Philosopher's Eye, stood at the foot of the Tower of Wisdom. This was connected to the largest tower by the library. Tar knew where to go from there, so he propelled Abeka toward it. The jabbo was keeping his pain at bay. His wounds seemed negligible despite their cruelty. Even his mind was clear. He felt more alive than ever.

A squad of men clad in sealskin cloaks ran along the foot of the tower and formed a wall in front of the Philosopher's Eye. They were armed with long spears. His sword was of little use, but he didn't break stride. Abeka screamed for him to stop. He ignored her. If he died today, let his monument be a hill of her enemies.

Even as he reached the speartips, the rank of sealskins burst apart: the tower guard, alerted by the screaming, attacked them from behind. A furious fight broke out and churned all around him. Where was Abeka?

Then he glimpsed her. A soldier in livery he didn't recognize had his hand clapped over her mouth, and with several confederates was dragging her through a concealed doorway in the wall.

Tar rushed after her. The last of the sealskins were dead, so the tower guards came after him—assuming he was one of the enemy.

With the flat of his sword, he caught the door before it closed behind the kidnappers. He followed the commotion in front of him down a poorly-lit hallway.

Some semblance of reason returned to him. If the men who had stolen Abeka hadn't killed her yet, they weren't with the sealskins. If he fought them, they might kill her by mistake. Instead of catching up, he kept himself out of sight and followed them through the labyrinth of servant's passages he'd explored before. Abeka, he was pleased to hear, was giving them a difficult time. She had plenty of fight in her.

Then a door closed and the noises ceased. When he came around the corner, he saw four doorways. He opened the nearest one. Stairs going upward. Silence. She hadn't gone that way.

As he reached for the second door handle, he heard the sound of running boots some distance behind him. The palace guards were on his trail. Before he could open the door and hide, it swung wide—concealing him behind it— and another squad of sealskins came through. They went straight for another of the doors, heedless of Tar's presence.

As the last of them closed the door behind him, the palace guards arrived. These men didn't see the sealskins— only Tar. They charged. With seconds to spare, he dived through the remaining door— and crashed into the backs of yet another team of sealskins already there.

· · ·

SURPRISE WAS ON HIS SIDE, although Tar was as surprised as they were. For the first time in his life, he met an enemy with a naked blade and didn't kill anyone. Instead, he used his momentum to plow through them—the space was confined and they were facing the wrong way—and flung himself through the curtains behind which they were concealed.

In this manner, Tar saw the Meridian Chamber for the first time, plummeting head-over-heels over a balcony railing twenty feet above the main floor. He bounced off a large golden statue of some minor god and crash-landed on a gaggle of shaven-headed acolytes of High Priest Shadra. They usefully broke his fall, and he was on his feet in a moment.

At a glance, he saw the space itself, the main floor ringed by three galleries above. The precious metal decoration on every surface glowed bright due to the sunlight pouring in from the open wall at one end. Beyond that was the king's private harbor, thick with luxurious ships.

He also saw the room was packed with people, all of them staring at him. Most of these were heavily armed. There were soldiers with the same unfamiliar livery as the men who had grabbed Abeka outside the tower, bald scythe-wielding warrior monks of High Priest Shadra's personal guard, and a great many knights.

All of this Tar took in before a second had passed. He saw Abeka was there, too, flanked by soldiers who held her arms. Facing her were High Priest Shadra himself, and another man whose jeweled crown proclaimed him to be Duke Illusan of Okré.

Like everyone else, Abeka was staring at Tar.

The chamber was completely silent, except for the groans of a couple of the acolytes still on the floor.

"Defend the princess!" Tar shouted.

Even as he spoke, the sealskin army concealed all around

the upper galleries broke cover with a roar, flooding down the spiral stairs on every side. If there were fifty armed men below, there must have been three times as many of these disguised fighters. Unless everyone could fight like Tar, the princess was about to be butchered.

He rushed toward her, and the liveried men and monks closed ranks against him.

"He's my man," Abeka shouted over the din. "To me, Tar Yunkai!"

It was enough to get him through the forest of blades, and once again he found himself at Abeka's side with a bloody sword in his hand.

"Will you explain what's going on?" he asked her.

"I have no idea," she said.

There was no more time for talk. The tide of sealskins was pressing across the chamber. Tar joined the ranks of defenders, and with a monk on one side and a knight on the other, hurled himself into the fray.

42

Tar had never seen such pandemonium as reigned in the Meridian Chamber that day. It made the fight to capture the Cormorant look like a game of bounders.

Sealskins were firing springbows from the balconies into the struggling mass below; defenders shot up at the bowmen. The curling stairs ran with rivers of hot blood and wounded men fell screaming on every side. The richly carved metal walls and ornaments of the chamber amplified the din of combat until it was like nails driven into the ears. The stench of blood, bowels, and sweat mingled with incense and perfume.

Tar kept fighting with all the strength he had left. The knight beside him dropped, then the monk, and still he fought on. But the sheer number of enemies was pressing the defenders back into an angle of the room from which there was no escape. He knew they were doomed, and did not regret it. He was going to die for something he believed in. Few had such an opportunity.

The dwindling number of men around him formed a

compact wall with the princess, duke, and high priest behind it. Tar saw that Abeka had gotten herself a knife. If she couldn't live as a princess, she would die like a queen.

"Die with a red blade," he said to her.

The distraction almost cost Tar his life. Only a quick-armed monk's scythe stopped the axe from reaching his neck. Tar killed the axeman with an upward thrust and took the axe. With a weapon in each fist, he rejoined the fight. Then he was surrounded by sealskins, and knew his Gods had tired of him.

He was wrong. Tall, lean figures appeared all around them like phantoms. Their knives were so swift they could not be seen. They shouted in a language he'd heard before—Krait sometimes used it. He was grateful for their deadly skill. With these reinforcements, the princess might survive another minute or two.

Then a furious new cry broke out, and from the harbor, the Emperor's Guard charged into the Meridian Chamber. These men were fresh, well-armored, and berserk with rage, the finest fighters of all the Atlantean armies. As they crashed like a tsunami into the sealskins, the battle became a rout, and the floor was sloshing with gore and guts. Tar found himself without an enemy to fight. All those near him had been swept away in the onslaught.

"THIS WILL CEASE *immediately!*" roared a voice as big and deep as the sea.

It boomed over the din of combat and smote the platinum vaults overhead. A few eyes, then many eyes, then all eyes fell upon the man who had stomped into the Meridian Chamber after the main force. He was dressed like a common sailor and held an iron cutlass in his hand. Every inch of his crimson sash was embroidered with voyages.

Everyone but the men in the Emperor's Guard fell to their knees and pressed their brows against the bloody floor—Abeka, Duke Illusan, and High Priest Shadra included. The surviving sealskins dropped their weapons and prostrated themselves flat. Even the wounded and dying stifled their cries in the presence of this tall, fierce man with thunder coming out of his mouth.

Tar looked around himself at all the upraised asses. He had never seen a combat end like this.

"Who are you?" He asked the fierce man.

Abeka rose first, as was her prerogative by rank:

"This is my father," she said. "Great King of Atlantis and Emperor of All Her Domains and of Her Mother the Sea."

43

Tar was at a loss for words.

"Your daughter talks about you a lot," he said.

The king glared at him.

"Who the fuck is this impertinent shark turd?"

"Don't be angry, Father," Abeka said, and took his oakhard hand. "He does not understand our customs. It's one of the best things about him."

"You *know* this—this ambulatory walrus pecker?"

"Yes, Father. He is my protector."

The king saw the fear and confusion on her face, and his anger fell away.

"My daughter, I am so happy to see you. You are a woman now."

He threw his arms around her. Then he released her and turned his attention to the chamber.

"Now, by the bright red asshole of the Midwinter Lion, what is happening here? There is about to be a mass execution, and I would prefer the correct persons die. But it is not fucking imperative. Brother Duke Illusan! What is all this? Is this your doing?"

Illusan rose, performing a deep Atlantean bow.

"Half of it is, Brother King."

"Half? I see quarters. Your men, the priests, and these tall folk must be Libagoro. Who are those sealskin pricks?"

"I know not, Brother King."

"Why the fuck are you even here?"

"He intended to marry me, Your Majesty," said Abeka.

She looked at her uncle with such contempt as only the daughter of a warrior-king could muster. She continued:

"It was your brother Duke Illusan who kidnapped and imprisoned me. This man Tar set me free, and kept me safe and alive until today."

The king regarded her from beneath his black brows, then turned to his brother again.

"Is this true?"

Illusan again touched his forehead to the blood-speckled floor.

"It's not as simple as that," he said, but did not elaborate.

"Duke Illusan," the king said, "you caused my absence, and then took advantage of it."

"Not at all, Brother King."

"Brother King no longer. I strip you of your titles. You are banished from Atlantis and her domains. "

Ex-Duke Illusan got to his feet unsteadily, only bringing himself to a royal posture by degrees.

"I live and die by your command," he croaked.

"You're fucking right you do," said the king. "Remember that."

Illusan hurried out. A few of his men followed; the rest stayed behind. Emperor first, duke second. They stripped off their liveried sleeves and sashes and tossed them on the floor.

"Bring me one of those scurvy pelt-wearing shitheads," The king commanded.

Four of Illusan's ex-soldiers eagerly marched up to the nearest seal-skinned man. They escorted him back, and he was so well-trained that he fell into step with them and marched in the same manner up to the king. He stood at attention.

The king loomed over the soldier like an avalanche.

"You're trained in royal parade maneuvers," the king said. "Whose man are you?"

"I cannot say, your Majesty, but live and die at your command."

"So you'll die before you tell me?"

"I live and d—"

The king's heavy cutlass split the man's skull.

"Bring me another," he said.

"Enough," said a high, quivering voice. "They're mine."

The Queen of Atlantis stepped onto a balcony that overlooked the blood-painted Meridian Chamber floor. A dozen of her men in their customary livery took their places beside her.

The king pointed at one of the sealskins.

"You: is that true?"

"Her Majesty could never lie, your Majesty. I live and die at your command."

"Then kill yourself," the king said.

He turned his attention to the balcony again, even as the renegade shoved his dagger into his own heart.

The queen stood against the balustrade like a ship's figurehead. Her sleeves were pearl-threaded galaxies of spider lace, her silken skirts pleated a thousand times. Her skin was entirely powdered in gold, her feet with ruby dust. The white hair at her temples was thick with diamonds and the rest was black with beads of jet.

She would always be beautiful, but her beauty was

dimmed by the stain of habitual misery, as sulfur darkens silver.

"So these are your men," the king said to her. "Were they here to stop this nonsense? Tell me that's why they're here, to stop the wedding."

"Don't be a sentimental fool," she replied. "They are here at my command—to kill our daughter."

44

A gasp of shock went up around the room. Everyone scrambled to their feet. At that moment, several of the sealskins spontaneously tried to flee. They were cut down within two strides.

The king didn't notice any of this. He was staring up at his wife, stupefied.

"At your command?" he said, in a much smaller voice than usual.

"What choice had I?" the queen demanded. "Your traitorous brother wants to spew his seed into our daughter's womb. Then, when you die early—which you surely will—he takes the throne alongside our daughter instead of me, and their accursed offspring follow suit."

"Then stop *him*, don't kill her!"

"He'll only try again, Husband. And again and again until he has her—she is the key to the throne. So the key must be destroyed."

"That's a thin excuse. You've always hated her," the king said. "This hatred has wounded your heart."

"No," came a familiar voice. "That would be mine."

There was the clatter-crack of a harpoon bow and the hiss of its missile flying to the mark.

The Queen was dead, pinned through her sternum to the sculptured wall.

Krait was on the opposite balcony—the one from which Tar had jumped earlier.

"One of her boys killed my lover," she said, and threw the weapon aside to draw her sword. "What goes the fuck around, comes the fuck around."

The king was as transfixed by his wife's death as she was by Krait's harpoon.

Then he snapped out of it:

"Kill that bitch at once."

His men swarmed up the spiral stairs toward Krait. She nimbly climbed a tapestry to the balcony above, then threw herself behind a white marble sculpture of a sea tiger. Springbow bolts snapped and shattered across the stone, but Krait was untouched. She ducked out of sight.

Tar didn't know what to do. His partner would soon be dead unless he acted. Krait was a madwoman, but he was bound to her by his word of honor.

"Remember me well," Tar said to Abeka. "And forgive me."

He was kneading the grip of his axe with both hands.

"Tar, don't do it," Abeka cried.

It was too late.

He rushed toward the fray. Krait was cornered up high and running out of cover, and had begun to collect glancing wounds from the soldiers closest to her.

The imperial guards were not expecting an attack from behind. Tar vaulted up the stairs and hewed wildly into them, creating a gap in their ranks.

"To me!" he called to Krait.

She took the opening and jumped over the balcony to

the one below. Tar was right behind her. They jumped again to the main floor, crashing down on tables laden with seafood delicacies. Before their foes could regroup, they charged toward the sea entrance, which the guards had left nearly unattended in their rush to join the battle.

Two of the king's men went down, and the pirates were outside in the daylight, sprinting for the water's edge with bits of appetizers flying off them.

It was a similar maneuver to the one that had gotten the Barracuda through the Atlantean line.

"You incompetent whoresons," the king snarled at his men, and snatched a guard's springbow out of his hands.

He aimed it at the fleeing pair. Tar's back was foremost in his view.

Abeka stepped in front of the weapon. She looked into her father's face with all the authority of her birth.

"You may not kill him," she said.

"Have you *also* lost your wits?" he whispered to Abeka.

His springbow was still pointed at her throat.

The Libagoro surrounded them. Their knives were tucked away. One of the assassins gently disarmed the king, then handed the weapon back to the guard from whom it had come.

This Libagoro, even taller and thinner than Krait, now dropped to her knee in front of Abeka.

"I am Nightshade Milk, knife-mistress of this diplomatic mission. I live and die at your command, Great Princess. Our score is now settled."

"Score? You owe me nothing," Abeka said. "You never did."

"We owe you peace. A friendship burdened with such a weighty obligation can never thrive. Now our debts are settled, may we prosper one and all."

"You have my heartfelt thanks, and the thanks of my father," Abeka said, and bade Nightshade Milk to rise.

The king broke in:

"How the fuck did you people know to be here? I only got word my girl was in Atlantis two days ago."

Nightshade Milk bowed.

"One of our broken-knife daughters, Krait Venom, sent word by sailors whose ship she had scuttled. She Who Won The War With a Single Stroke was in danger, and her danger would be greatest when she entered this palace. We have been concealed here for five days, awaiting her arrival."

"You came to stop the wedding?" the king said.

"Only to keep Princess Abeka safe. We didn't know of this wedding."

"Then I owe Krait Venom a great deal for her service to the crown. Bring her forth."

"We cannot, Emperor. It is she who slew the Queen."

The king's eyes bulged.

"I want those two fugitives skinned and brined alive," he shouted at his men. "That Krait woman and the idiot."

"Father," Abeka said, "It is for his sake that I spoiled your shot."

"I have not seen you in years," he said. "We haven't even properly greeted each other. And the first thing you do is step in front of my bow for some bumptious twist of gristle?"

"I'll tell you everything, Father. But I beg, before it is too late—"

A guard hurried up to the king and bowed, interrupting:

"Your Majesty, they dived into the harbor. We have not found them yet. We are closing the canal gates and will seal off the palace."

"I want them alive. They have some suffering to do."

"Father, you must listen to me," Abeka said.

"Take this foolish girl to my quarters," the king said to

the guard. "You and fifty men. A hundred men. Not so much as a mosquito gets past you. Now, as for you Libagoro—"

He stopped in mid-command.

The assassins were no longer there.

Here ends the second tale

ABOUT THE AUTHOR

Fenix 'Nix' Harper-Jones lives in rural northwestern France. When she isn't writing, Nix spends her time restoring an old, long-neglected farmhouse, initiating disastrous romances, and conducting site surveys for l'*Institut National de Recherches Archéologiques Préventives*. This is her second novel.